C000244000

Tucholsky Wagner Zola Scott Sydow Freud Schlegel
Turgenev Wallace Fonatne

Twain Walther von der Vogelweide Fouqué Friedrich II. von Preußen
Weber Freiligrath Frey
Fechner Ernst
Fichte Weiße Rose von Fallersleben Kant Frommel
Richthofen
Engels Fielding Hölderlin
Fehrs Faber Flaubert Eichendorff Tacitus Dumas
Eliasberg Ebner Eschenbach
Feuerbach Maximilian I. von Habsburg Fock Eliot Zweig
Ewald Vergil
Goethe London
Mendelssohn Balzac Shakespeare Elisabeth von Österreich
Dostojewski Ganghofer
Trackl Lichtenberg Rathenau Doyle Gjellerup
Stevenson Hambruch
Mommsen Tolstoi Lenz Droste-Hülshoff
Thoma Hanrieder
Dach Verne von Arnim Hägele Hauff Humboldt
Reuter
Karrillon Garschin Rousseau Hagen Hauptmann Gautier
Defoe Baudelaire
Damaschke Descartes Hebbel
Hegel Kussmaul Herder
Wolfram von Eschenbach Schopenhauer
Darwin Dickens Rilke George
Bronner Melville Grimm Jerome
Campe Horváth Aristoteles Bebel Proust
Bismarck Vigny Barlach Voltaire Federer Herodot
Gengenbach Heine
Storm Casanova Tersteegen Gilm Grillparzer Georgy
Chamberlain Lessing Langbein Gryphius
Brentano Lafontaine
Strachwitz Claudius Schiller Kralik Iffland Sokrates
Katharina II. von Rußland Bellamy Schilling
Gerstäcker Raabe Gibbon Tschechow
Löns Hesse Hoffmann Gogol Wilde Gleim Vulpius
Luther Heym Hofmannsthal Klee Hölty Morgenstern
Roth Heyse Klopstock Goedicke
Luxemburg Puschkin Homer Kleist
La Roche Horaz Mörike Musil
Machiavelli Kierkegaard Kraft Kraus
Navarra Aurel Musset
Nestroy Marie de France Lamprecht Kind Kirchhoff Hugo Moltke
Nietzsche Nansen Laotse Ipsen Liebknecht
Marx Ringelnatz
von Ossietzky Lassalle Gorki Klett Leibniz
May vom Stein Lawrence Irving
Petalozzi
Platon Knigge
Sachs Pückler Michelangelo Kock Kafka
Poe Liebermann
de Sade Praetorius Mistral Zetkin Korolenko

Finnish Legends for English Children

R. Eivind

Imprint

This book is part of the TREDITION CLASSICS series.

Author: R. Eivind
Cover design: toepferschumann, Berlin (Germany)

Publisher: tradition GmbH, Hamburg (Germany)
ISBN: 978-3-8491-6197-2

www.tredition.com
www.tredition.de

PREFACE

THE following stories cover almost all of the songs of the Kalevala, the epic of the Finnish people. They will lead the English child into a new region in the fairy world, yet one where he will recognise many an old friend in a new form. The very fact that they *do* open up a new portion of the world of the marvellous, will, it is hoped, render them all the more acceptable, and perhaps, when the child who reads them grows up to manhood, will inspire an actual interest in the race that has composed them.

And this race and their land will repay study, for nowhere will one find a more beautiful land than Finland, nor a braver, truer, and more liberty-loving people than p. vi the Finns, although, alas, their love for liberty may soon be reduced to an apparently hopeless longing for a lost ideal. For the iron hand of Russian despotism has already begun to close on Finland with its relentless grasp, and, in spite of former oaths and promises from the Russian Tsars, the future of Finland looks blacker and blacker as time goes on. Yet it is often the unforeseen that happens, and let us trust that this may be so in Finland's case, and that a brighter future may soon dawn, and the dark clouds that now are threatening may be once more dispersed.

In these stories Mr. T. M. Crawford's metrical translation of the Kalevala has been quite closely followed, even to the adoption of his Anglicised, or rather Anglo-Swedish, forms for proper names, though in some instances the original Finnish form has been reverted to. This was done reluctantly, but the actual Finnish forms would seem formidable to children in many instances, and would probably be pronounced even farther from the original than as they are given here. It is to be hoped, moreover, that those who may now read these stories will later on p. vii read an actual translation of the Kalevala, and this is an additional reason for adopting the terminology of the only English translation as yet made. [1]

[1] A Finnish newspaper recently states that Mr. C. is now at work on an improved translation.

As this book is only intended for children, it would be out of place to discuss the age, etc., of the Kalevala. Only it would seem proper to state, that while the incantations and some other portions of the text are certainly very old, some of them no doubt dating from a period prior to the separation of the Finns and Hungarians, yet, as Professor Yrj□□oskinen remarks, "The Kalevala in its present state is without doubt the work of the *Karelian* tribe of Finns, and probably dates from *after* their arrival in Northern and North-Western Russia." This will of itself largely justify the making *Kalevala* synonymous with the present *Finland*, *Pohjola* with the present Lapland, Karjala with the present *Karjala* (Anglice, *Karelia*) in South-Eastern Finland, etc. But even if this were not so, yet the advantage of such localisation in a book for children is of itself obvious.

As the land and people with which the stories are concerned is so unknown to p. viii English children, it has seemed best to have some sort of introduction and framework in which to present them, and therefore "Father Mikko" was chosen as the story-teller.

If this little volume may in any degree awake some interest in the Finnish people its author will be amply satisfied, and its end will have been attained.

R. EIVIND.

April 1893.

CONTENTS

Father Mikko
The World's Creation and the Birth of Wainamoinen
The Planting of the Trees
Wainamoinen and Youkahainen
Aino's Fate
Wainamoinen's Search for Aino
Wainamoinen's Unlucky Journey
Wainamoinen's Rescue
The Rainbow-Maiden
Ilmarinen Forges the Sampo
Lemminkainen and Kyllikki
Kyllikki's Broken Vow
Lemminkainen's Second Wooing
Lemminkainen's Death
Lemminkainen's Restoration
Wainamoinen's Boat-Building
Wainamoinen Finds the Lost Words
The Rival Suitors
Ilmarinen's Wooing
The Brewing of Beer
Ilmarinen's Wedding Feast
The Origin of the Serpent
The Unwelcome Guest
The Isle of Refuge
The Frost-Fiend
Kullervo's Birth
Kullervo and Ilmarinen's Wife
Kullervo's Life and Death
Ilmarinen's Bride of Gold
Ilmarinen's Fruitless Wooing
Wainamoinen's Expedition and the Birth of the Kantele
(Harp)
The Capture of the Sampo
The Sampo is Lost in the Sea
The Birth of the Second Kantele
Louhi Attempts Revenge

Louhi Steals the Sun, the Moon, and Fire
The Restoration of the Sun and Moon
Mariatta and Wainamoinen's Departure

TABLE OF PROPER NAMES
WITH PRONUNCIATION

Ahti (āch-tee). Another name for Lemminkainen.

Ahto (āch-to). God of the sea.

Ainikki (ā뷁ik-kĕe). Sister of Lemminkainen.

Aino (ā뷁o). Sister of Youkahainen.

Annikki (an-nĭk-kee). Sister of Ilmarinen.

Hisi (hee-see). Evil spirit; also called Lempo.

Iku Turso (ee-koo-tūr-so). A sea-monster.

Ilmarinen (il-mā-ree-nĕn). The famous smith.

Ilmatar (il-mă-tar). A daughter of the ether, mother of Wainamoinen.

Imatra (ee-mā-tră). Celebrated waterfall on the river Wuoksi, near Viborg.

Kalerwoinen (kal-er-woi-nĕn) (*or* Kalervo). Father of Kullervo.

Kalevala (kā-lay-vā-lā). The land of heroes. The home of the Finns. The name of the Finnish epic poem.

Karjala (kar-yā-lā). The home of a Finnish tribe—a portion of Finland (called also *Karelen* in Swedish).

p. xiv

Kullervo (kŭl-ler-vō). Slayer of the Rainbow-maiden.

Kura (kū-ra). Ahti's companion to the Northland.

Lakko (lāk-ko). Ilmarinen's mother.

Lemminkainen (lĕm-min-kā뷁nēn). Also called *Ahti*. Son of *Lempo*.

Lempo (lĕm-po). Same as *Hisi*; also the father of Lemminkainen.

Louhi (loo-chee). Mistress of Pohjola.

Lowjatar (low-yā-tar). Tuoni's daughter; mother of the nine diseases.

Lylikki (ly-lĭk-kee). Maker of snow-shoes in Pohjola.

Mana (mā-nā). Also called Tuoni; god of death.

Manala (mā-nā-lā). Also called Tuonela; the abode of Mana; the Deathland.

Mariatta (Mar-ĭat-tă). The virgin mother of Wainamoinen's conqueror.

Mielikki (meay-lĭk-kee). The forest-goddess.

Osmotar (os-mō-tar). The wise maiden who first made beer.

Otso (ot-sō). The bear.

Piltti (pilt-tee). Mariatta's maid-servant.

Pohjola (pōch-yō-lā). The Northland.

Ruotus (rū-ō-tŭs). A man who gives Mariatta shelter in his stable.

Sampo (sām-pō). The magic mill forged by Ilmarinen, which brought wealth and happiness to its possessor.

Suonetar (swō-nĕ-tăr). The goddess of the veins.

Suoyatar (swō-yă-tăr). The mother of the serpent.

Tapio (ta-pĕ-ō). The forest-god.

p. xv

Tuonela (tuo-nay-la). The abode of Tuoni; the Deathland; Manala.

Tuonetar (tuo-nay-tar). The goddess of Tuonela.

Tuoni (tuo-nee). The god of the Deathland; Mana.

Ukko (ūk-k(ō). The greatest god of the Finns.

Untamo (ūn-tā-mō). Kalervo's brother.

Wainamoinen (wā벽nā-moy-nĕn). The chief hero of the Kalevala; son of Kap縷/p>

Wipunen (wĭ-pū-nen). The dead magician from whom Wainamoinen obtained the three lost words.

Wirokannas (wee-rō-kan-năs). The priest who baptized Mariatta's son.

Wuoksi (wūōk-see). A river in South-Eastern Finland, connecting Lakes Saima and Ladoga.

Youkahainen (yoo-ka-chä▥něn). A great minstrel and magician of Pohjola.

Remarks. — The Finnish *h* is pronounced as a guttural; nearly as Ger. *ch* in *ich*. This is represented by *ch* in the above list.

Every vowel should be pronounced by itself — not run together so as to make a totally different resultant sound, *e.g. Aino* should be pronounced not *ī-nō*, but *ä-ee-nō*, the *ä* and *ee* being close together, with the greatest stress upon the *ä*, etc.

i corresponds to English *y* in *year*.

LIST OF ILLUSTRATIONS

Finnish Kota
Sleighing in Finland   *Facing page*
Interior of Lapp Hut   "
A Lapland Wizard   "
Lapp Women in Holiday Costume   "
Mimi in Holiday Dress   "
A Waterfall   "

FATHER MIKKO

FAR up in the ice-bound north, where the sun is almost invisible in winter, and where the summer nights are bright as day, there lies a land which we call Finland; but the people who live there call it *Suomenmaa* now, and long, long ago they used to call it *Kalevala* (which means the *land of heroes*). And north of Finland lies Lapland, which the Finns now call *Lappi*, but in the olden days they called it Pohjola (that is, *Northland*). There the night lasts for whole weeks and months about Christmas, and in the summer again they have no night at all for many weeks. For more than half the year their country is wrapped in snow and frost, and yet they are both of them a kind-hearted people, and among the most honest and truthful in the world.

p. 2

One dark winter's day an old man was driving in a sledge through the fir forest in the northern part of Finland. He was so well wrapped up in sheep-skin robes that he looked more like a huge bundle of rugs, with a cord round the middle, than anything else, and the great white sheep-skin cap which he wore hid all the upper part of his face, while the lower part was buried in the high collar of his coat. All one could see was a pair of bright blue eyes with frost-fringed eyelashes, blinking at the snow that was thrown up every now and then by his horse's feet.

He was a travelling merchant from away up in the north-western part of Russia, and had been in southern Finland to sell his wares, at the winter fairs that are held every year in the Finnish towns and villages. Now he was on his way home, and had come up through Kuopio, and had got on past Kajana already, but now it had just begun to snow, and as the storm grew worse, he pressed on to reach the cabin of a friend who lived not far ahead; and he intended to stay there until the storm should subside and the weather be fit for travelling once more.

It was not long before he reached the cabin, and getting out of his sledge slowly, being stiff from the cold and the cramped position, he knocked on the door with his p. 3 whip-handle. It was opened at once, and he was invited in without even waiting to see who it was, and was given the welcome that is always given in that country to a wearied traveller. But when he had taken his wraps off there was a general cry of recognition, and a second even more hearty welcome.

'Welcome, Father Mikko!'

'What good fortune has brought you hither?'

'Come up to the fire,' and a chorus of cries from two little children, who greeted 'Pappa Mikko' with delight as an old and welcome acquaintance. Then the father of the family went out and attended to Father Mikko's horse and sledge, and in a few minutes was back again and joined the old man by the fire. Next his wife brought out the brandy-bottle and two glasses, and after her husband had filled them, he and Father Mikko drank each other's health very formally, for that is the first thing one must do when a guest comes in that country. You must touch your glass against your friend's, and say 'good health,' and raising it to your lips drink it straight off, and all the time you must look each other straight in the eyes.

When this important formality was finished the four members of the family and Father Mikko made themselves comfortable p. 4 around the fire, and they began to ask him how things had prospered with him since they had seen him last, and to tell him about themselves—how Erik, the father of the family, had been sick, and the harvest had been extra good that year, and one of the cows had a calf, and all the things that happen to people in the country.

And then he told them of what was going on in the towns where he had been, and how every one was beginning to get ready for Christmas. And he turned to the two little children and told them about the children in the towns—how they had had such a lovely time at 'Little Christmas,' [2] at the house he was staying in. How the little ones had a tiny little tree with wee wax candles on it exactly like the big tree they were to have at Christmas, and how, when he left, all the children had begun to be impatient for Christmas Eve, with its presents and Christmas fish and porridge.

[2] A children's festival about one week before the real Christmas.

After the old man had ended his account it was dinner-time, and they all ate with splendid appetites, while Father Mikko declared that the herring and potatoes and rye-bread and beer made a far better dinner than any he had had in the big cities in the south—not even in Helsingfors had he had a better. Then when dinner was over, and they p. 5 had all gathered round the fire again, little Mimi climbed up into 'Pappa Mikko's' lap, and begged him to tell them '*all* the stories he had ever heard, from the very beginning of the world all the way down.' And her father and mother joined with her in her request, for in their land even the grown-up people have not become too grand to listen to stories. As for the little boy, Antero, he was too shy to say anything; but he was so much interested to hear 'Pappa Mikko' that he actually forgot to nibble away at a piece of candy which 'Pappa Mikko' had brought from St. Michel.

The old man smiled, for he was always asked for stories wherever he went—he was a famous story-teller—and, stroking little Mimi's hair gently, he looked at the group around the fire before replying. There was Erik, the father, a broad-shouldered man, with a dark, weather-beaten face and rather a sad look, as so many of his countrymen have. His face showed that his struggle in the world had not been easy, for he had to be working from the time he got up until he went to bed; and then when the harvest had been bad, and the winter much longer than usual, and everything seemed to go wrong— ah! it was so hard then to see the mother and the little ones have only bark-bread to eat, and not always enough p. 6 of that, and one winter they had had nothing else for months. Erik wouldn't have minded for himself, but for them ...! Ah well, that was all over now; he had been able at last to save up a little sum of money, and the harvests were extra good this year, and he had bought Mother Stina a cloak for Christmas! Just think of it—a fine cloak, all the way from the fair at Kuopio!

And next to Erik sat his wife Stina, a short, fat little woman, with such a merry face and happy-looking eyes that you could hardly believe that she had lived on anything but the best herring and potatoes and rye-bread all her life. Close by her side was her little boy Antero, who was only seven years old, and in his eagerness for the stories to commence he still held his piece of candy in his hand without tasting it.

Then there was little Mimi in Father Mikko's lap. She was nearly ten years old, and was not a pretty little girl; but she had very lovely soft brown eyes and curly flaxen hair, and a quiet, demure manner of her own, and her mother declared that when she grew up she would be able to spin and weave and cook better than any other girl in the parish, and that the young man that should get her Mimi for a wife would get a real treasure.

SLEIGHING IN FINLAND.

And lastly, there was Father Mikko himself, an old man over sixty, yet strong and p. 7 hearty, with a long gray beard and gray hair, and eyes that fairly twinkled with good humour. You could hardly see his mouth for his beard and moustache, and certainly his nose *was* a little too small and turned up at the end to be exactly handsome, and his cheek-bones *did* stand out a little too high; but yet everybody, young and old, liked him, and his famous stories made him a welcome guest wherever he came.

So Father Mikko lit his queer little pipe, and settled down comfortably with Mimi in his lap, and a glass of beer at his side to refresh himself with when he grew weary of talking. There was only the firelight in the room, and as the flames roared up the chimney they cast a warm, cosy light over the whole room, and made them all feel so comfortable that they thanked God in their hearts in their simple way, because they had so many blessings and comforts when such a storm was raging outside that it shook the house and drifted the snow up higher than the doors and windows.

Then Father Mikko began, and this is the first story that he told them.

THE WORLD'S CREATION AND THE BIRTH OF WAINAMOINEN

LONG, long ago, before this world was made, there lived a lovely maiden called Ilmatar, the daughter of the Ether. She lived in the air—there were only air and water then—but at length she grew tired of always being in the air, and came down and floated on the surface of the water. Suddenly, as she lay there, there came a mighty storm-wind, and poor Ilmatar was tossed about helplessly on the waves, until at length the wind died down and the waves became still, and Ilmatar, worn out by the violence of the tempest, sank beneath the waters.

Then a magic spell overpowered her, and she swam on and on vainly seeking to rise above the waters, but always unable to do so. Seven hundred long weary years she swam thus, until one day she could not bear it any longer, and cried out: 'Woe is me p. 9 that I have fallen from my happy home in the air, and cannot now rise above the surface of the waters. O great Ukko, [3] ruler of the skies, come and aid me in my sorrow!'

[3] The chief god of the Finns before they became Christians.

No sooner had she ended her appeal to Ukko than a lovely duck flew down out of the sky, and hovered over the waters looking for a place to alight; but it found none. Then Ilmatar raised her knees above the water, so that the duck might rest upon them; and no sooner did the duck spy them than it flew towards them and, without even stopping to rest, began to build a nest upon them.

When the nest was finished, the duck laid in it six golden eggs, and a seventh of iron, and sat upon them to hatch them. Three days the duck sat on the eggs, and all the while the water around Ilmatar's knees grew hotter and hotter, and her knees began to burn as if they were on fire. The pain was so great that it caused her to tremble all over, and her quivering shook the nest off her knees, and the eggs all fell to the bottom of the ocean and broke in pieces. But these pieces came together into two parts and grew to a huge size, and the upper one became the arched heavens above us, and the lower one our world itself. From the white part of the egg came the moonbeams, and from the yolk the bright sunshine. p. 10

At last the unfortunate Ilmatar was able to raise her head out of the waters, and she then began to create the land. Wherever she put her hand there arose a lovely hill, and where she stepped she made a lake. Where she dived below the surface are the deep places of the ocean, where she turned her head towards the land there grew deep bays and inlets, and where she floated on her back she made the hidden rocks and reefs where so many ships and lives have been lost. Thus the islands and the rocks and the firm land were created.

After the land was made Wainamoinen was born, but he was not born a child, but a full-grown man, full of wisdom and magic power. For seven whole years he swam about in the ocean, and in the eighth he left the water and stepped upon the dry land. Thus was the birth of Wainamoinen, the wonderful magician.

'Ah!' said little Mimi, with a sigh of relief, 'I was afraid you weren't going to tell us about Wainamoinen at all.'

And then Father Mikko went on again.

THE PLANTING OF THE TREES

WAINAMOINEN lived for many years upon the island on which he had first landed from the sea, pondering how he should plant the trees and make the mighty forests grow. At length he thought of Sampsa, the first-born son of the plains, and he sent for him to do the sowing. So Sampsa came and scattered abroad the seeds of all the trees and plants that are now on the earth, — firs and pine-trees on the hills, alders, lindens, and willows in the lowlands, and bushes and hawthorn in the secluded nooks.

Soon all the trees had grown up and become great forests, and the hawthorns were covered with berries. Only the acorn lay quiet in the ground and refused to sprout. Wainamoinen watched seven days and nights to see if it would begin to grow, but it lay perfectly still. Just then he saw ocean p. 12 maidens on the shore, cutting grass and raking it into heaps. And as he watched them there came a great giant out of the sea and pressed the heaps into such tight bundles that the grass caught fire and burnt to ashes. Then the giant took an acorn and planted it in the ashes, and almost instantly it began to sprout, and a tree shot up and grew and grew until it became a mighty oak, whose top was far above the clouds, and whose branches shut out the light of the Sun and the Moon and the stars.

When Wainamoinen saw how the oak had shut off all the light from the earth, he was as deeply perplexed how to get rid of it, as he had been before to make it grow. So he prayed to his mother Ilmatar to grant him power to overthrow this mighty tree, so that the sun might shine once more on the plains of Kalevala.

No sooner had he asked Ilmatar for help than there stepped out of the sea a tiny man no bigger than one's finger, dressed in cap, gloves, and clothes of copper, and carrying a small copper hatchet in his belt. Wainamoinen asked him who he was, and the tiny man replied: 'I am a mighty ocean-hero, and am come to cut down the oak-tree.' But Wainamoinen began to laugh at the idea of so little a man being able to cut down so huge a tree.

But even while Wainamoinen was laugh p. 13 ing, the dwarf grew all at once into a great giant, whose head was higher than the clouds, and whose long beard fell down to his knees. The giant began to whet his axe on a huge piece of rock, and before he had finished he had worn out six blocks of the hardest rock and seven of the softest sandstone. Then he strode up to the tree and began to cut it down. When the third blow had fallen the fire flew from his axe and from the tree; and before he had time to strike a fourth blow, the tree tottered and fell, covering the whole earth, north, south, east, and west, with broken fragments. And those who picked up pieces of the branches received good fortune; those who found pieces of the top became mighty magicians; and those who found the leaves gained lasting happiness.

And then the sunlight came once more to Kalevala, and all things grew and flourished, only the barley had not yet been planted. Now Wainamoinen had found seven magic barley-grains as he was wandering on the seashore one day, and he took these and was about to plant them; but the titmouse stopped him, saying: 'The magic barley will not grow unless thou first cut down and burn the forest, and then plant the seeds in the wood-ashes.'

So Wainamoinen cut down the trees as the titmouse had said, only he left p. 14 the birch-trees standing. After all the rest were cut down an eagle flew down, and, alighting on a birch-tree, asked why all the others had been destroyed, but the birches left. And Wainamoinen answered that he had left them for the birds to build their nests on, and for the eagle to rest on, and for the sacred cuckoo to sit in and sing. The eagle was so pleased at this that he kindled a fire amongst the other trees for Wainamoinen, and they were all burnt except the birches.

Wainamoinen then brought forth the seven magic barley-seeds from his skin-pouch, and sowed them in the ashes, and as he sowed he prayed to great Ukko to send warm rains from the south to make the seeds sprout. And the rain came, and the barley grew so fast that in seven days the crop was almost ripe.

WAINAMOINEN AND YOUKAHAINEN

 THUS Wainamoinen finished his labours and began to lead a happy life on the plains of Kalevala. He passed his evenings singing of the deeds of days gone by and stories of the creation, until his fame as a great singer spread far and wide in all directions.

At this time, far off in the dismal Northland, there lived a young and famous singer and magician named Youkahainen. He was sitting one day at a feast with his friends, when some one came and told about the famous singer Wainamoinen, and how he was a sweeter singer and a more powerful magician than any one else in the world. This filled Youkahainen's heart with envy, and he vowed to hasten off to the south and to enter into a contest with Wainamoinen to see if he could not beat him.

His mother tried to persuade him not to p. 16 go, but in vain, and he made ready for the journey, declaring that he would sing such magic songs as would turn old Wainamoinen into stone. Then he brought out his noble steed and harnessed him to a golden sledge, and then jumping in, he gave the steed a cut with his pearl-handled whip, and dashed off towards Kalevala. On the evening of the third day he drew near to Wainamoinen's home, and there he met Wainamoinen himself driving along the highway.

Now Youkahainen was too proud to turn out of the road for any one, and so their sledges dashed together and were smashed to pieces, and the harnesses became all twisted up together. Then Wainamoinen said: 'Who art thou, O foolish youth, that thou drivest so badly that thou hast run into my sledge and broken it to pieces?' And Youkahainen answered proudly: 'I am Youkahainen, and have come hither to beat the old magician Wainamoinen in singing and in magic.'

Wainamoinen then told him who he was, and accepted the challenge, and so the contest began. But Youkahainen soon found that he was no match for his opponent, and at length he cried out in anger: 'If I cannot beat thee at singing and in magic, at least I can conquer thee with my bright sword.' p. 17

Wainamoinen answered that he would not fight so weak an opponent, and then Youkahainen declared that he was a coward and afraid to fight. At last these taunts made Wainamoinen so angry that he could not restrain himself any longer, and he began to sing. He sang such wondrous spells that the mountains and the rocks began to tremble, and the sea was upheaved as if by a great storm. Youkahainen stood transfixed, and as Wainamoinen went on singing his sledge was changed to brushwood and the reins to willow branches, the pearl-handled whip became a reed, and his steed was transformed into a rock in the water, and all the harness into seaweed. And still the old magician sang his magic spells, and Youkahainen's gaily-painted bow became a rainbow in the sky, his feathered arrows flew away as hawks and eagles, and his dog was turned to a stone at his feet. His cap turned into a curling mist, his clothing into white clouds, and his jewel-set girdle into stars.

And at length the spell began to take effect on Youkahainen himself. Slowly, slowly he felt himself sinking into a quicksand, and all his struggles to escape were in vain. When he had sunk up to his waist he began to beg for mercy, and cried out: 'O great Wainamoinen, thou art the greatest of all magicians. Release me, I p. 18 beg, from this quicksand, and I will give thee two magic bows. One is so strong that only the very strongest men can draw it, and the other a child can shoot.'

But Wainamoinen refused the bows and sank Youkahainen still deeper. And as he sank, Youkahainen kept begging for mercy, and offering first two magic boats, and then two magic steeds that could carry any burden, and finally all his gold and silver and his harvests, but Wainamoinen would not even listen to him. At length Youkahainen had sunk so far that his mouth began to be filled with water and mud, and he cried out as a last hope: 'O mighty Wainamoinen, if thou wilt release me I will give thee my sister Aino as thy bride.'

This was the ransom that Wainamoinen had been waiting for, for Aino was famous for her beauty and loveliness of character, and so he released poor Youkahainen and gave him back his sledge and everything just as it had been before. And when it was all ready Youkahainen jumped into it and drove off home without saying a word.

When he reached home he drove so carelessly that his sledge was broken to pieces against the gate-posts, and he left the broken sledge there and walked straight into the house with hanging head, and at p. 19 first would not answer any of his family's questions. At length he said: 'Dearest mother, there is cause enough for my grief, for I have had to promise the aged Wainamoinen my dear sister Aino as his bride.' But his mother arose joyfully and clapped her hands and said: 'That is no reason to be sad, my dear son, for I have longed for many years that this very thing should happen—that Aino should have so brave and wise a husband as Wainamoinen.'

So the mother told the news to Aino, but when she heard it she wept for three whole days and nights and refused to be comforted, saying to her mother: 'Why should this great sorrow come to me, dear mother, for now I shall no longer be able to adorn my golden hair with jewels, but must hide it all beneath the ugly cap that wives have to wear. All the golden sunshine and the silver moonlight will go from my life.'

But her mother tried to comfort her by telling her that the sun and moon would shine even more brightly in her new home than in her old, and that Kalevala was a land of flowers.

'I think Aino was very stupid not to want to leave that horrid Lapland,' said Mimi; 'but then I suppose she didn't know p. 20 what a beautiful country ours is,' she added thoughtfully.

Here Antero, who only cared for the stories, mustered up enough courage to ask Pappa Mikko to go on, which the old man did at once.

AINO'S FATE

THE next morning the lovely Aino went early to the forest to gather birch shoots and tassels. After she had finished gathering them she hastened off towards home, but as she was going along the path near the border of the woods she met Wainamoinen, who began thus:

'Aino, fairest maid of the north, do not wear thy gold and pearls for others, but only for me; wear for me alone thy golden tresses.'

'Not for thee,' Aino replied, 'nor for others either, will I wear my jewels. I need them no longer; I would rather wear the plainest clothing and live upon a crust of bread, if only I might live for ever with my mother.'

And as she said this she tore off her jewels and the ribbons from her hair, and p. 22 threw them from her into the bushes, and then she hurried home, weeping. At the door of the dairy sat her mother, skimming milk. When she saw Aino weeping she asked her what it was that troubled her. Aino, in reply, told her all that had happened in the forest, and how she had thrown away from her all her ornaments.

Her mother, to comfort her, told her to go to a hill-top near by and open the storehouse there, and there in the largest room, in the largest box in that room, she would find six golden girdles and seven rainbow-tinted dresses, made by the daughters of the Moon and of the Sun. 'When I was young,' her mother said, 'I was out upon the hills one day seeking berries. And by chance I overheard the daughters of the Sun and Moon as they were weaving and spinning upon the borders of the clouds above the fir-forest. I went nearer to them, and crept up on a hill within speaking distance of them. Then I began to beseech them, saying: "Give some of your silver, lovely daughters of the Moon, to a poor but worthy maid;

and I beg you, daughters of the Sun, give me some of your gold." And then the Moon's daughters gave me silver from their treasure, and the Sun's daughters gave me gold that I might adorn my hair and forehead. I hastened joyfully home with my treasures to my mother's house, p. 23 and for three days I wore them. Then I took them off and laid them in boxes, and I have never seen them since. But now, my daughter, go and adorn thyself with gold and silk ribbons; put a necklace of pearls around thy neck, and a golden cross upon thy bosom; dress thyself in pure white linen; put on the richest frock that is there and tie it with a belt of gold; put silk stockings on thy feet and the finest of shoes. Then come back to us that we may admire thee, for thou wilt be more beautiful than the sunlight, more lovely than the moonbeams.'

But Aino would not be consoled, and kept on weeping. 'How happy I was in my childhood,' she sang, 'when I used to roam the fields and gather flowers, but now my heart is full of grief and all my life is filled with darkness. It would have been better for me if I had died a child;—then my mother would have wept a little, and my father and sisters and brothers mourned a little while, and then all their sorrow would have been ended.'

Aino wept for three days more, and then her mother once more asked her why she wept so, and Aino replied: 'I weep, O mother, because thou hast promised me to the aged Wainamoinen, to be his comforter and caretaker in his old age. Far better if thou hadst sent me to the bottom of the sea, p. 24 to live with the fishes and to become a mermaid and ride on the waves. This had been far better than to be an old man's slave and darling.'

When she had said this she left her mother and hastened to the storehouse on the hill. There she opened the largest box and took off six lids, and at the bottom found six golden belts and seven silk dresses. She chose the best of all the treasures there and adorned herself like a queen, with rings and jewels and gold ornaments of every sort.

When she was fully arrayed she left the storehouse and wandered over fields and meadows and on through the dim and gloomy fir-forest, singing as she went: 'Woe is me, poor broken-hearted Aino! My grief is so heavy that I can no longer live. I must leave this earth and go to Manala, the country of departed spirits. Father, mother, brothers, sisters, weep for me no longer, for I am going to live beneath the sea, in the lovely grottos, on a couch of sea-moss.'

For three long weary days Aino wandered, and as the cold night came on she at last reached the seashore. There she sank down, weary, on a rock, and sat there alone in the black night, listening to the solemn music of the wind and the waves, as they sang her funeral melody. When at p. 25 last the day dawned Aino beheld three water-maidens sitting on a rock by the sea. She hastened to them, weeping, and then began to take off all her ornaments and lay them carefully away. When at length she had laid all her gold and silver decorations on the ground, she took the ribbons from her hair and hung them in a tree, and then laid her silken dress over one of the branches and plunged into the sea. At a distance she saw a lovely rock of all the colours of the rainbow, shining in the golden sunlight. She swam up and climbed upon it to rest. But suddenly the rock began to sway, and with a loud crash it fell to the bottom of the sea, carrying with it the unhappy Aino. And as she sank down she sang a last sad farewell to all her dear ones at home—a song that was so sweet and mournful that the wild beasts heard it, and were so touched by it that they resolved to send a messenger to tell her parents what had happened.

So the animals held a council, and first the bear was proposed as messenger, but they were afraid he would eat the cattle. Next came the wolf, but they feared that he might eat the sheep. Then the fox was proposed, but then he might eat the chickens. So at length the hare was chosen to bear the sad tidings, and he promised to perform his office faithfully.

He ran like the wind, and soon reached p. 26 Aino's home. There he found no one in the house, but on going to the door of the bath-cabin he found some servants there making birch brooms. They had no sooner caught sight of him than they threatened to roast him and eat him, but he replied: 'Do not think I have come hither to let you roast me. For I come with sad tidings to tell you of the flight of Aino and how she died. The rainbow-coloured stone sank with her to the bottom of the sea, and she perished, singing like a lovely song-bird.

There she sleeps in the caverns at the bottom of the sea, and on the shore she has left her silken dress and all her gold and jewels.'

When these tidings came to her mother the bitter tears poured from her eyes, and she sang, 'O all other mothers, listen: never try to force your daughters from the house they long to stay in, unto husbands whom they love not. Thus I drove away my daughter, Aino, fairest in the Northland.'

Singing thus she sat and wept, and the tears trickled down until they reached her shoes, and began to flow out over the ground. Here they formed three little streams, which flowed on and grew larger and larger until they became roaring torrents, and in each torrent was a great waterfall. And in the midst of the waterfalls rose three huge rocky p. 27 pillars, and on the rocks were three green hills, and on each of the hills was a birch-tree, and on each tree sat a cuckoo. And all three sang together. And the first one sang 'Love! O Love!' for three whole moons, mourning for the dead maiden. And the second sang 'Suitor! Suitor!' wailing six long moons for the unhappy suitor. And the third sang sadly 'Consolation! Consolation!' never ending all his life long for the comfort of the broken-hearted mother.

Mother Stina looked at little Mimi very solemnly when this story was ended, as if she wondered whether she herself would ever need to take to heart the warning of Aino's mother. But no one said anything, and Father Mikko continued on with the next story.

WAINAMOINEN'S SEARCH FOR AINO

 WHEN the news reached Wainamoinen he began to weep most bitterly, and the tears fell all that day and night; but the next day he hastened to the water's edge and prayed to the god of dreams to tell him where the water-gods dwelt. And the dream-god answered him lazily, and told him where the island was around which the sea-gods and the mermaids lived.

Then Wainamoinen hastened to his boat-house, and chose a copper boat, and in it placed fishing lines and hooks and nets, and when all was ready he rowed off swiftly towards the forest-covered island which the dream-god had told him of. No sooner had he arrived there than he began to fish, using a line of silver and a hook of gold. But for many days he fished in vain, yet p. 29 still he persevered. At last one day a wondrous fish was caught, and it played about and struggled a long time until at length it was exhausted, and the hero landed it in the boat.

When Wainamoinen saw it he was astonished at its beauty, but after gazing at it for some time he drew out his knife and was about to cut it up ready for eating. But no sooner had he touched the fish with his knife than it leapt from the bottom of the boat and dived under the water. Then it rose again out of his reach and said to him: 'O ancient minstrel, I did not come hither to be eaten by thee, merely to give thee food for a day.'

'Why didst thou come then?' asked Wainamoinen.

'I came, O minstrel, to rest in thine arms and to be thy companion and wife for ever,' the fish replied; 'to keep thy home in order and to do whatever thou pleased. For I am not a fish; I am no salmon of the Northern Seas, but Youkahainen's youngest sister. I am the one thou wert fishing for—Aino, whom thou lovest. Once thou wert wise, but now art foolish, cruel. Thou didst not know enough to keep me, but wouldst eat me for thy dinner!'

Then Wainamoinen begged her to return to him, but the fish replied: 'Nevermore will Aino's spirit come to thee to be so p. 30 treated,' and as it spoke the fish dived out of sight.

Still Wainamoinen did not give up, but took out his nets and began dragging the waters. And he dragged all the waters in the lands of Lapland and of Kalevala, and caught fish of every sort, only Aino, now the water-maiden, never came into his net. 'Fool that I am,' he said at length, 'surely I was once wise, had at least a bit of wisdom, but now all my power has left me. For I have had Aino in my boat, but did not know until too late that I had even caught her.' And with these words he gave up his search and set off to his home in Kalevala. And on his way he mourned that the joyous song of the sacred cuckoo had ceased, and he sang: 'I shall never learn the secret how to live and prosper. If only my ancient mother were still living, she could give me good advice that this sorrow might leave me.'

Then his mother awoke from her tomb in the depths and spoke to him: 'Thy mother was but sleeping, and I'll now advise thee how this sorrow may pass over. Go at once to the Northland, where dwell wise and lovely maidens, far lovelier than Aino. Take one of them for thy wife; she will make thee happy and be an honour to thy home.'

p. 31

'I don't think he had much of a heart if he could be consoled so easily as all that,' said Mother Stina, a little indignantly.

'Wait and you shall see,' said old Father Mikko with a smile; and he continued.

WAINAMOINEN'S UNLUCKY JOURNEY

 WAINAMOINEN made ready for a journey to the Northland, to the land of cold winters and of little sunshine, where he was to seek a wife. He saddled his swift steed, and mounting, started towards the north. On and on he went upon his magic steed, galloping over the plains of Kalevala. And when he came to the shores of the wide sea, he did not halt, but galloped on over the water without even so much as wetting a hoof of his magic courser.

But wicked Youkahainen hated Wainamoinen for what he had done when he defeated him in magic, and so he made ready a bow of steel. He painted it with many bright colours and trimmed it with gold and silver and copper. Then he chose the strongest sinews from the stag, and at p. 33 length the great bow was ready. On the back was painted a courser, at each end a colt, near the bend a sleeping maiden, near the notch a running hare. And after that he cut some arrows out of oak, put tips of sharpened copper on them, and five feathers on the end. Then he hardened the arrows and steeped them in the blood of snakes and the poison of the adder to give them magic power.

When all was ready Youkahainen went out to wait for his enemy. For many days and nights he watched in vain, but still he did not weary, and at last one day at dawn he saw what seemed to be a black cloud on the waters. But by his magic art he knew that it was Wainamoinen on his magic steed. Then he went after his bow, but his mother stopped him and asked him whom he meant to shoot with his bow and poisoned arrows. Youkahainen replied: 'I have made this mighty bow and these poisoned arrows for the old magician Wainamoinen, that I may destroy my rival.'

His mother reproved him, saying, 'If thou slayest Wainamoinen all our joy will vanish, all the singing and music will die with him. It is better that we have his magic music in this world than to have it all go to the underground world Manala, where the spirits of the dead dwell.' p. 34

Youkahainen hesitated for a moment, but then envy and hatred filled his heart, and he replied: 'Even though all joy and pleasure vanish from the world, yet will I shoot this rival singer, let the end be what it will.'

With these words he hastened out and took his stand in a thicket near the shore. He chose the three strongest arrows from his quiver, and selecting the best among these three, he laid it against the string and aimed at Wainamoinen's heart. And as he still waited for him to come nearer, he sang this incantation: 'Be elastic, bow-string mine, swiftly fly, O oaken arrow, swift as light, O poisoned arrow, to the heart of Wainamoinen. If my hand too low shall aim thee, may the gods direct thee higher. If mine eye too high shall aim thee, may the gods direct thee lower.'

Then he let the arrow fly, but it flew over Wainamoinen's head and pierced and scattered the clouds above. Again he shot a second, but it flew too low and penetrated to the depths of the sea. Then he aimed the third, and it flew from his bow swift as lightning. Straight forward it flew, and struck the magic steed full in the shoulder so that Wainamoinen was plunged headlong into the waves. And then arose a mighty storm-wind, and the old magician was carried far out into the wide open sea.

But Youkahainen believed that he had p. 35 killed his rival, and so went home, rejoicing and singing as he went. And his mother asked him, 'Hast thou slain great Wainamoinen?' and he replied, 'I have slain old Wainamoinen. Into the salt sea he plunged headlong, and the old magician is now at the bottom of the deep.'

But his mother replied: 'Woe to earth for what thou hast done. Joy and singing are gone for ever, for thou hast slain the great wise singer, thou hast slain the joy of Kalevala.'

All his listeners seemed very much dissatisfied at the turn the story had taken, so Father Mikko hastened to assure them that Wainamoinen was not really dead, and then he began the next story.

WAINAMOINEN'S RESCUE

BUT Wainamoinen was not dead, but swam on for eight days and seven nights trying to reach land. And when the evening of the eighth day came and still no land was in sight, he began to grow tired and to despair of ever getting out alive.

But just then he spied an eagle of wonderful size flying towards him from the west. And the eagle flew up to him and asked who he was and how he had come there in the ocean.

And Wainamoinen replied: 'I am Wainamoinen, the great singer and magician. I had left my home for the distant Northland, and as I galloped over the ocean and neared the shore, the wicked Youkahainen killed my steed with his magic arrows, and I was cast headlong into the waters. And then a mighty wind arose and drove me farther p. 37 and ever farther out to sea, and now I have been struggling with the winds and waves for eight long weary days, and I fear that I shall perish of cold and hunger before I reach any land.'

INTERIOR OF LAPP HUT.

The eagle replied: 'Do not be discouraged, but seat thyself upon my back and I will carry thee to land, for I have not forgotten the day when thou left the birch-trees standing for the birds to sing in and the eagle to rest on.'

So Wainamoinen climbed upon the eagle's broad back and seated himself securely there, and off the eagle flew, straight to the nearest land. There on the shore of the dismal Northland the eagle left him, and flew off to join his mate.

Wainamoinen found himself upon a bare, rocky point of land, without a trace of human life about it, nor any path through the woods by which it was surrounded. And he wept bitterly, for he was far from home, covered with wounds from his battle with the winds and waters, and faint with hunger: three days and three nights he wept without ceasing.

Now the fair and lovely daughter of old Louhi had laid a wager with the Sun, that she would rise before him the next morning. And so she did, and had time to shear six lambs before the Sun had left his couch beneath the ocean. And after this she p. 38 swept up the floor of the stable with a birch broom, and collecting the sweepings on a copper shovel, she carried them to the meadow near the sea-shore. There she heard the sound of some one weeping, and hastening back she told her mother of it.

Then Louhi, ancient mistress of the Northland, hurried out from her house and down to the seashore. There she heard the sound of weeping, and quickly pushed off from the shore in a boat and rowed to where the weeping Wainamoinen sat.

When she came to him she said to him: 'What folly hast thou done to be in so sad a state?'

Wainamoinen replied: 'It is indeed folly that has brought me into this trouble. I was happy enough at home before I went on this expedition.'

Then Louhi asked him to tell her who he was of all the great heroes.

Wainamoinen replied: 'Formerly I was honoured as a great singer and magician: I was called the "Singer of Kalevala," the wise Wainamoinen.'

Then Louhi said: 'Rise, O hero, from thy lowly couch among the willows, come with me to my home and there tell me the story of thy adventures.' So she took the starving hero into her boat and rowed him to the shore, and took him to her house. There she gave him food, and the warmth p. 39 and rest and shelter soon restored to him all his strength. Then Louhi asked him to relate his adventures, and he told her all that had happened to him.

When he had finished Louhi said to him: 'Weep no more, Wainamoinen, for thou shalt be welcome in our homes, thou shalt live with us and eat our salmon and other fish.'

Wainamoinen thanked her for her kindness, but added: 'One's own country and table and home are the best and dearest. May the great god, Ukko, the Creator, grant that I may once more reach my dear home and country. It is better to drink clear water from a birchen cup in one's own home, than in foreign lands to drink the richest liquors from the golden beakers of strangers.'

Then Louhi asked him: 'What reward wilt thou give me, if I carry thee back to thy beloved home, to the plains of Kalevala?'

Wainamoinen asked her what reward she would consider suffi-cient, whether gold or silver treasures, but Louhi answered: 'I ask not for gold or silver, O wise Wainamoinen, but canst thou forge for me the magic Sampo, with its lid of many colours, the magic mill that grinds out flour on one side, and salt from another side, and turns out money from the third? I will give p. 40 thee, too, my daughter, as a reward, to be thy wife and to care for thy home.'

But Wainamoinen answered sadly: 'I cannot forge for thee the magic Sampo, but take me to my country and I will send thee Il-marinen, who will make it for thee, and wed thy lovely daughter. Ilmarinen is a wondrous smith; he it was who forged the heavens, and so perfectly did he do it that we cannot see a single mark of the hammer on them.'

Louhi replied: 'Only to him who can forge the magic Sampo for me will I give my daughter.' Then she harnessed up her sledge and put Wainamoinen in it and made him all ready for his journey home. And as he started off she spoke these words to him: 'Do not raise thy eyes to the heavens, do not look upward while the day lasts, before the evening star has risen, or a terrible misfortune will happen to you.'

Then Wainamoinen drove off, and his heart grew light as he left the dismal Northland behind him on his way to Kalevala.

THE RAINBOW-MAIDEN

 THE fair Rainbow-maiden, Louhi's daughter, sat upon a rainbow in the heavens, and was clad in the most splendid dress of gold and silver. She was busy weaving golden webs of wonderful beauty, using a shuttle of gold and a silver weaving-comb.

As Wainamoinen came swiftly along the way which led from the dark and dismal Northland to the plains of Kalevala, before he had gone far on his way he heard in the sky above him the humming of the Rainbow-maiden's loom. Without thinking of old Louhi's warning, he looked up and beheld the maiden seated on the gorgeous rainbow weaving beauteous cloths. No sooner had he seen the lovely maiden than he stopped, and calling to her asked her to come to his sledge. p. 42

The Rainbow-maiden replied: 'Tell me what thou wishest of me.'

'Thou shalt come with me,' Wainamoinen replied, 'to bake me honey-biscuit, to fill my cup with foaming beer, to sing beside my table, to be a queen within my home in the land of Kalevala.'

But the maiden replied: 'Yesterday I went at twilight to the flowery meadows. There I heard a thrush singing, and I asked him, "Tell me, pretty song-bird, how shall I live most happily, as a maiden in my father's home or as a wife by my husband's side?" And the bird sang in reply, "The summer days are bright and warm, and so is a maiden's freedom; the winter is cold and dark, and so are the lives of married women. They are like dogs chained in a kennel, no favours are given to wives."'

But Wainamoinen answered the maiden: 'The thrush sings only nonsense. Maidens are treated like little children, but wives are like queens. Come to my sledge, O maiden, for I am not the least among heroes, nor am I ignorant of magic. Come, and I will make thee my wife and queen in Kalevala.'

Then the Rainbow-maiden promised to be his wife if he would split a golden hair with a knife that had no edge, and take a bird's egg from the nest with a snare that no one could see. Wainamoinen did both these things, and then begged her to come to p. 43 his sledge, for he had done what she asked.

But she set another task for him, telling him she would marry him if he could peel a block of sandstone and cut a whip-handle from ice without making a single splinter. And Wainamoinen did both these things, but still the maiden refused to go until he had performed a third task. This was to make from the splinters of her distaff a little ship, and to launch it into the water without touching it.

Then Wainamoinen took the pieces of her distaff and set to work. He took them to a mountain from which he got the iron for his work, and for three days he laboured with hatchet and hammer. But on the evening of the third day a wicked spirit, Lempo, caught his hatchet as he raised it up, and turned it as it fell, so that it hit a rock and broke in fragments, and one of the pieces flew into the magician's knee, and cut it, so that the blood poured out.

Then Wainamoinen began to sing a magic incantation to stop the blood from flowing, but his magic was powerless against the evil Lempo, and he could not stop the blood. Then he gathered certain herbs with wonderful powers, and put them on the wound, but still he could not heal it up, for Lempo's spell was too powerful for his magic. So he got into his sledge again, and drove off at a p. 44 gallop to seek for help. Soon he came to a place where the road branched off in three directions. He chose the left-hand one, and galloped on till he reached a house. When he went to the door he found only a boy and a baby inside, and when he had told them what he wanted, the boy said, 'There is no one here that can help thee, but take the middle road, and perhaps thou wilt find help.'

So off he galloped to where the roads branched off, and then along the middle one to another house. There he found an old witch lying on the floor, but she gave him the same answer that the boy had done, and sent him to the right-hand road.

On this road he came to another cottage, where an old man with a long gray beard was sitting by the fire. And when Wainamoinen told him of his trouble, the old man replied, 'Greater things have been done by but three of the magic words; water has been turned to land, and land to water.' On hearing this answer Wainamoinen rose from his sledge and went into the cottage, and seated himself there. And all this time his knee was bleeding, so that the blood was enough to fill seven huge birchen pots.

Then the old man asked him who he was, and bade him sing to him the origin [4] of the p. 45 iron that had wounded him so, and Wainamoinen related the following story of how iron was first made:

[4] For they believed that a magic song that told the *origin* of any trouble would also cure it.

Long ago after there were air and water, fire was born, and after the fire came iron. Ukko, the creator, rubbed his hands upon his left knee, and there arose thence three lovely maidens, who were the mothers of iron and steel. These three maidens walked forth on the clouds, and from their bosoms ran the milk of iron, down unto the clouds and thence down upon the earth. Ukko's eldest daughter cast black milk over the river-beds, and the second cast white milk over the hills and mountains, and the third red milk over the lakes and oceans; and from the black milk grew the soft black iron-ore; from the white milk the lighter-coloured ore; and from the red milk the brittle red iron-ore.

After the iron had lain in peace for a while, Fire came to visit his brother Iron and tried to eat him up. Then Iron ran from him and took refuge in the swamps and marshes, and that is how we now find iron-ore hidden in the marshes.

Then was born the great smith, Ilmarinen, and the next morning after he was born he built his smithy on a hill near the marshland. There he found the hidden iron-ore, and carried it to his smithy and put it in the furnace to be smelted. And Ilmarinen had p. 46 not blown more than three strokes of the bellows before the iron began to grow soft as dough. But then Iron cried out to him, 'Take me from this furnace, Ilmarinen, save me from this cruel torture!' for the heat of the fire had grown unbearable.

'Thou art not hurt, but only a little frightened,' Ilmarinen replied; 'but I will take thee out, and thou shalt be a great warrior and slay many heroes.'

But Iron swore by the hammer and anvil, 'I will injure trees and mountains, but I'll never kill the heroes. I will be men's servant and their tool, but will not serve for weapons.'

So Ilmarinen put the iron on his anvil, and made from it many fine things and tools of every kind. But he could not harden the iron into steel, though he pondered over it for a long time. He made a lye from birch-ashes and water to harden the iron in, but it was all in vain.

Just then a little bee came flying up, and Ilmarinen begged him to bring honey from all the flowers in the meadows, that he might put it in the water and so harden the iron to steel. But a hornet, one of the servants of the evil spirit Lempo, was sitting on the roof and overheard Ilmarinen's words. And the hornet flew off and collected all the evil charms he could find — the hissing of serpents, the venom of adders, the poison of p. 47 spiders, the stings of every insect — and brought them to Ilmarinen. He thought that the bee had come and brought him honey from the meadows, and so mixed all these poisons with the water in which he was to plunge the iron. And when he thrust the iron into the poisoned water it was turned to hard steel, but the poisons made it forget its oath and grow hard-hearted, and it began to wound men and cause their blood to flow in streams. This was the origin of steel and iron.

When Wainamoinen had finished, the old man rose from the hearth and began an incantation to make the wound close up. First he cursed Iron that it had become so wicked, and then he bade the blood cease to flow by the power of his magic. And as he went on he prayed to great Ukko that if this magic incantation should not prove sufficient, Ukko himself would come and stop the wound.

By the time he had finished his words of magic the blood ceased flowing from the wound. Then the old man sent his son to make a healing salve out of herbs, to take away the soreness from Wainamoinen's knee.

First the youth made a salve from oak-bark and young shoots, and many sorts of healing grasses. Three days and three nights he steeped them in a copper kettle, p. 48 but when he had finished the salve would not do. Then he added still other healing herbs, and steeped it for three days more, and at last it was ready. First he tried it on a birch-tree that had been broken down by wicked Lempo. He rubbed the salve on the broken branches and said: 'With this salve I anoint thee, recover, O birch-tree, and grow more beautiful than ever!'

And the tree grew together and became more beautiful and strong than ever before. Then he tried the salve on broken granite boulders and on fissures in the mountains, and it was so powerful that it closed them all together as if they had never existed. After this he hurried home and gave the magic salve to his father, and told him what he had done with it.

The old man anointed Wainamoinen's knee with it, saying: 'Do not rely on thine own virtue or power, but in thy creator's strength; do not speak with thine own wisdom, but with great Ukko's. Whatever in thee is good comes from Ukko.'

No sooner had the old man put on the salve and said these words, than Wainamoinen was seized with a terrible pain, and lay rolling and writhing on the floor in agony. But the old man bandaged up his knee with a silken bandage, and prayed to Ukko to come to his assistance.

And suddenly the pain left Wainamoinen p. 49 and his knee became as strong and well as ever. Then he raised his eyes in gratitude to heaven and prayed thus to Ukko: 'Praise to thee, my Creator, for the aid that thou hast given me. For thou hast banished all my pain and trouble. O all ye people of Kalevala, both those now living and those to come, boast not of the work that ye have done but give to God the praise, for the great Ukko alone can make all things perfect, Ukko is the one master!'

There was a moment's pause, and then little Mimi said that she was so glad Wainamoinen was well again, and asked Father Mikko to tell them what happened to him next. But the old man answered that he must have a *little* time to breathe at least. So he filled his pipe again and lighted it, and Erik brought up some more beer, and they sat and smoked and drank beer and chatted for a while.

Then, when he felt rested once more, Father Mikko obeyed Mimi's urgent request and began again to tell them how Wainamoinen got home, and what happened afterwards.

ILMARINEN FORGES THE SAMPO

NO sooner was Wainamoinen cured of his wound than he put his sledge in order and drove off at lightning speed towards Kalevala. For three days he journeyed over hills and valleys, over marshes and meadows, and on the evening of the third day he reached the land of Kalevala once again.

There, on the border line he halted, and began a magic song. And as he sang a fir-tree began to grow from the earth, and kept on growing until its top had grown up above the clouds and reached to the stars. When the tree had finished growing, Wainamoinen sang another magic song, so that the moon was caught fast in the tree's branches and obliged to shine there until Wainamoinen should reverse his spell. And then by another spell he made the stars of the Great Bear fast in the tree-top, and then p. 51 jumped into his sledge and drove on again to his home, with his cap set awry on his head, mourning because he had promised to send Ilmarinen back to the Northland, to forge the magic Sampo as his ransom.

As he drove on he came to Ilmarinen's smithy, and he stopped and went in to him. Ilmarinen welcomed him and asked where he had been so long, and what had happened to him.

Then Wainamoinen told him of his journey to the Northland, and all the dangers he had gone through, and he added: 'In a village there I saw a maiden, who is the fairest in all the Northland. All there sing her praises, for her forehead shines like the rainbow and her face is fair as the golden moonlight. She is more beautiful than the sun and all the stars together, but she will not marry any suitor. But do thou go, dear Ilmarinen, and see her wondrous beauty; forge the magic Sampo for her mother and then thou shalt win this lovely maiden to be thy wife.'

But Ilmarinen replied: 'O cunning Wainamoinen, I know that thou hast promised me as a ransom for thyself. But I will never go

65

to that gloomy country, nor do I care for thy beautiful maiden; I will not go for all the maids in Pohjola.'

Wainamoinen answered: 'But I can tell p. 52 thee of still greater wonders, for I have seen a giant fir-tree growing on the border of our own country; its top is higher than the clouds, and in its branches shine the moon and the Great Bear.'

'I will not believe thy wonderful story,' replied Ilmarinen, 'until I see the tree with my own eyes and the moon and stars shining in it.'

'Come with me,' said Wainamoinen, 'and I will show thee that I speak the truth.' So off they set to see the wondrous tree. When they had come to it Wainamoinen asked Ilmarinen to climb the tree and to bring down the moon and stars, and he at once began to climb up towards them.

But, while he was climbing, the fir-tree spoke to him, saying: 'Foolish hero, why hast thou so little knowledge as to try to steal the moon from my branches?' No sooner had the tree said these words to Ilmarinen, than Wainamoinen sang a magic spell, calling up a great storm-wind, and saying to it: 'O storm-wind, take Ilmarinen and carry him in thy airy vessel to the dark and dismal Northland.'

And the storm-wind came and heaped up the clouds so that they formed a boat, and seizing Ilmarinen from the tree it placed him in the clouds and rushed off to the north, carrying clouds and all with it. On and on he sailed, rising higher than the p. 53 moon, tossed about by the wind, until at last he came to the Northland and the storm-wind set him down in Louhi's courtyard.

Old toothless Louhi saw him as he alighted, and asked him: 'Who art thou that comest through the air, riding on the storm-wind? Hast thou ever met the great smith Ilmarinen, for I have long been waiting for him to come and forge the magic Sampo for me.'

'I do indeed know him well,' he replied, 'for I myself am Ilmarinen.'

At these words Louhi hurried into the house and told her youngest daughter to dress herself in all her most splendid clothes and ornaments, for Ilmarinen was come to make the Sampo for them. So the maiden chose her loveliest silken dresses, and placed a circlet of copper round her brow, a golden girdle round her waist, and pearls about her neck, and in her hair she twisted threads of gold and silver. When she was dressed she looked, with her rosy red cheeks and bright sparkling eyes, more lovely than any other maiden in all the Northland, and then she hurried to the hall to meet Ilmarinen.

Louhi went to Ilmarinen and led him into the house, where there was a feast spread ready for him. She gave him the best seat at the table, and the choicest p. 54 viands to eat, and gave him everything he wished for. Then she asked him if he would forge the Sampo for her, and promised him, if he would, her fairest daughter as his wife.

Ilmarinen was charmed with her daughter's beauty, and he promised to do what she asked. But when he went to look for a place to work in, he could find no place, and not even so much as a pair of bellows to blow his fire with. Still he was not discouraged, but for three days he wandered about, looking for a place to build a workshop. On the evening of the third day he saw a huge rock that was suited for his purpose, and there he began to build. The first day he built the chimney and started a fire; the second day he made his bellows and put them in place; the third day he finished his furnace, and had all ready to begin his work.

Then Ilmarinen made a magic mixture of certain metals and put them in the bottom of the furnace. And he hired some of Louhi's men to work the bellows and keep putting fuel on the fire. Three long summer days the workmen blew the bellows, until at length the base rock began to blossom in flames from the magic heat.

On the evening of the first day Ilmarinen bent over the furnace and took out a magic bow. It gleamed like the moon, had a p. 55 shaft of copper and tips of silver, and was the most wonderful bow that had ever been made. But it would not rest satisfied unless it killed a warrior every day, and two on feast-days. So Ilmarinen broke it into pieces and threw them back into the furnace, and tried again to forge the Sampo.

On the evening of the second day he looked into the furnace and drew forth a magic vessel. It was all purple, save the ribs that were of gold and the vase of copper, and it was the most beautiful vessel that ever had been made. But wherever it went it always led men into quarrels and fights, so Ilmarinen broke it into pieces and threw it back into the furnace.

On the evening of the third day he took out of the furnace a magic heifer, with horns of gold and the most beautifully-shaped head. But she was ill-tempered and would not stay at home, but rushed through the forest and swamps and wasted all her milk on the ground. So Ilmarinen cut the magic heifer in pieces and threw them back into the furnace.

And on the fourth evening he took out a wonderful plough, the ploughshare of gold and the handles of silver and the beam of copper. But it ploughed up fields of barley and the richest meadows, so Ilmarinen threw it back into the furnace.

Then he drove away all his workmen, p. 56 and by his magic called up the storm-winds to blow his bellows. They came from the North and South and East and West, and they blew one day and then another and then a third, until the fire leapt out through the windows, the sparks flew from the door, and the smoke rose up and mingled with the clouds. And on the third evening Ilmarinen looked into the furnace and beheld the magic Sampo growing there. Quickly he took it out and placed it on his anvil, and taking a huge hammer the wonderful smith forged the luck-bringing Sampo. From one side it grinds out flour, and from the other salt, and from the third it coins out money. And the lid is all the colours of the rainbow, and as it rocks back and forth it grinds one measure for the day, and one for the market and one for the storehouse.

Then old Louhi joyfully took the luck-bringing Sampo and hid it in the hills of Lapland. She bound it with nine great locks, and by her witchcraft made three roots grow all around it, two deep beneath the mountains and one beneath the seashore.

And when he had finished the Sampo, Ilmarinen came to the lovely daughter of Louhi and asked her if she were ready now to be his wife. But she replied: 'If I should go with thee, and leave the Northland, all the birds would cease to sing. p. 57 No, never while I live will I give up my maiden freedom, lest all the birds should leave the forest and the mermaids leave the waters.'

So Ilmarinen had made the Sampo all in vain, and he was now far from home and had no way of returning. But Louhi came to him and asked him why he was grieving, and when she learned his trouble, and that he now wished to return to his own home, she provided him with a boat of copper. And when he had set sail she sent the north wind to carry him on his way, and on the evening of the third day he reached his home.

There Wainamoinen met him and asked if he had forged the magic Sampo. 'Yes,' replied Ilmarinen, 'I have forged the Sampo, with its lid of many colours. Louhi has the wondrous Sampo, but I have lost the beauteous maiden.'

'Ah!' said little Mimi, 'old Louhi's daughter was just as mean as could be, and of course she didn't keep her promise, because Lapps never can be good people.'

'Don't be too hard on the poor Lapps, my dear,' said Father Mikko, 'for you see this happened a great many hundreds of p. 58 years ago, and the whole world has grown better since then. But now we will leave Ilmarinen and Wainamoinen for a while, and I will tell you about the reckless Lemminkainen and his adventures.'

So the old man began as follows:

LEMMINKAINEN AND KYLLIKKI

LONG, long ago a son was born to Lempo, and he was named Lemminkainen, but some call him Ahti. He grew up amongst the islands and fed upon the salmon until he became a mighty man, handsome to look at and skilled in magic. But he was not as good as he was handsome—he had a wicked heart, and was more famous for his dancing than for great deeds.

Now at the time my story begins, there lived in the Northland a beautiful maiden named Kyllikki. She was so lovely that the Sun had begged her to marry his son and come and live with them. But she refused, and when the Moon came and besought her to marry her son, and the Evening Star sought her for his son, she refused them both. And after that came suitors from all the countries round about, p. 60 but the lovely Kyllikki would not marry one of them.

When Lemminkainen heard of this, he resolved that he would win her himself. But his aged mother tried to dissuade him, telling him that the maiden was of a higher family than his own, that all the Northland women would laugh at him, and then if he should try to punish them for their laughter, that the warriors of the Northland would fall on him and kill him. But all this did not make him change his mind, and he started off for the distant Northland.

When he came near to Kyllikki's home, all the women and maidens that saw him began to laugh at him because he looked so poor, and yet dared to try to win the fair Kyllikki's hand. When he heard them laughing, it made him so angry that he drove on without paying any attention to how he was driving, and when he came to the courtyard his sledge hit against the gate-post and broke to pieces, and threw him out into the snow.

He rose up angrier than ever, but all those around only laughed the harder at him, and made all manner of fun of him. Then they

71

offered him a place as a shepherd on the mountains. So Ahti became a shepherd, and spent all the days on the hills, but in the evenings he went to their dances, and when he had shown them what p. 61 a skilful dancer he was, he soon became a great favourite with all the women, and they began to praise him instead of laughing at him.

But fair Kyllikki alone would have nothing to do with him—would not even look at him in spite of all his endeavours to win her. At last she was tired out with his attentions, and told him that he had better return home, for she did not like him, and that so long as he stayed there she would not even look at him.

Still he did not go away, but waited until a chance came to carry out his new plan. About a month after this, all the maidens were met together for a dance in a glen among the hills, and among them was Kyllikki. Suddenly Lemminkainen came galloping up in his sledge and seized the fair Kyllikki as she was dancing with the rest, placed her in his sledge, and drove off like the whirlwind, and as he flew by the frightened maidens he cried out to them: 'Never tell that I have taken Kyllikki, or I will cast a magic spell over your lovers, so that they will all leave you and go off to the wars and will never come back to dance and make merry with you.'

But Kyllikki wept and begged Lemminkainen to give her back her freedom, saying, 'Oh, give me back my freedom, cruel Lemminkainen; let me return on foot to my p. 62 grieving father and mother. If thou wilt not let me go, O Ahti, I will curse thee and will call upon my seven valiant brothers to pursue and kill thee. Once I was happy among my people, but now all my joy has gone since thou hast come to torment me, O cruel-hearted Ahti!'

But all her words could not move Lemminkainen to release her. Then he said to her: 'Dearest maiden, fair Kyllikki, cease thy weeping and be joyful; I will never harm thee nor deceive thee. Why shouldst thou be sorrowful, for I have a lovely home and friends and riches, and thou shalt never need to labour. Do not despise me because my family is not mighty, for I have a good spear and a sharp sword, and with these I will gain greatness and power for thy sake.'

Then Kyllikki asked him: 'O Ahti, son of Lempo, wilt thou then be to me a faithful husband; wilt thou swear to me never to go to battle nor to strife of any sort?'

'I will swear upon my honour,' Lemminkainen replied, 'that I will never go to battle, if thou wilt promise in return never to go to dance in the village, however much thou mayst long for it.'

So the two swore before the great Ukko, Lemminkainen promising never to go to battle, and Kyllikki that she would never go to the village dances. And p. 63 then Lemminkainen rejoicing cracked his whip, and they galloped on like the wind over hills and valleys towards the plains of Kalevala.

As they came near to Lemminkainen's home, Kyllikki saw that it looked dreary and poor, and began to weep again, but Lemminkainen comforted her, telling her that now he would build a splendid mansion for her, and so she grew cheerful once more.

They drove up to his mother's cottage, and as they entered his mother asked him how he had fared. Ahti answered: 'I have well repaid the scorn of the Northland maidens, for I have brought the fairest of them with me in my sledge. I brought her well wrapt in bear-skins hither, to be my loving bride for ever. Beloved mother, make ready for us the best room and prepare a rich feast, that my bride may be content.'

His mother answered: 'Praised be gracious Ukko, that hath given me a daughter. Praise Ukko, my son, that thou hast won this lovely maiden, the pride of the Northland, who is purer than the snow, more graceful than the swan, and more beautiful than the stars. Let us make our dwelling larger, and decorate the walls most beautifully in honour of thy lovely bride, the fairest maid of all creation.'

KYLLIKKI'S BROKEN VOW

LEMMINKAINEN and Kyllikki lived together happily for many years, keeping the promises they had made to each other. But one day Lemminkainen had not come home from fishing by sunset, and then the longing to dance was more than Kyllikki could withstand, and she went into the village and joined the maidens in their dance.

As soon as Lemminkainen came home, his sister Ainikki came to him and told him how Kyllikki had broken her promise and had joined in the dance. Then Lemminkainen grew angry and sad at the same time, and he went to his mother and asked her to steep his clothing in the blood of serpents, for he was going off to battle since Kyllikki could not keep her vow.

Kyllikki tried to persuade him not to leave her, telling him that she had dreamt a p. 65 dream, in which she saw their home in flames and the fire bursting out through the doors and windows and roof. But Lemminkainen replied: 'I have no faith in women's dreams or maidens' vows. Bring me my copper armour, mother, for I long to get to the wars, to go to dismal Pohjola, there to win great stores of gold and silver.'

'Stay at home, my dear son,' his aged mother said, 'and drink the beer in our cellars, sitting peaceably by thine own hearth, for we have more than enough gold and silver. Only the other day, as our servants were ploughing the fields they came upon a chest of gold and silver buried in the ground — take this and be content.'

When all this had no effect upon Lemminkainen, his mother began to tell him of the magic of the Northland people, and that they would sing him into the fire so that he would be burnt to death. But he replied: 'Long ago three Lapland wizards tried to bewitch me, and employed their strongest spells against me, but I stood unmoved. Then I began my own magic songs, and before long I overcame them and sank them to the bottom of the sea, where they are still sleeping and the seaweed is growing through their hair and beards.'

Still his mother tried to stop him, and his wife Kyllikki begged his forgiveness in tears. He stood listening to them and brushing out p. 66 his long black hair, but at last he became impatient, and threw the brush from him and cried out: 'I will not stay, but keep that brush, and when ye see blood oozing from its bristles, then ye may know that some terrible misfortune has overtaken me.'

Saying this he left them and put on his armour and harnessed his steed into his sledge. Then he sang a song, calling on all the spirits of the woods and the mountains and the waters and on great Ukko himself to help him against the Northland wizards, and when his song was ended he drove off like the wind.

In the evening of the third day he reached a little village in the Northland. Here he drove into a courtyard and called out: 'Is there any one strong enough to attend to my horse and take care of my sledge.' There was a child playing on the floor of the house, and it replied that there was no one there to do it. Then Lemminkainen rode on to another house and asked the same question; and a man standing in the doorway replied: 'There are plenty here that are mighty enough not only to unharness thy steed, but to conquer thee and drive thee to thy home ere the sun has set.'

Then Lemminkainen told him that he would return and slay him, and so drove off to the highest house in the village. Here he cast a spell over the watch-dog, so that p. 67 he should not bark, and drove in. Then he struck on the ground with his whip, and from the ground there arose a vapour that concealed the sledge, and in the vapour was a dwarf that took his steed and unharnessed it and gave it food. But Lemminkainen went on into the house, having first made himself invisible. There he found a great many people singing and making merry, and by the fires the Northland wizards were seated. He made his way on, and then took on his own shape again and entered into the main hall, and cried out to those that were singing to be silent.

As soon as she saw him the mistress of the house ran up to him and asked him who he was, and how he had passed the watch-dog unnoticed. Then Lemminkainen told her who he was, and instantly began to weave his magic spells, while the lightning shot from his fur mantle and flames from his eyes. He sang them all under the power of his magic—some beneath the waters, some into the burning fire, some beneath the heaped-up mountains. Only one poor old man, who was blind and lame, did he leave untouched. And when the old man asked him why it was that he had alone been left, cruel Lemminkainen began to abuse him and to torment him with words, until the old man, Nasshut, grew almost wild with anger, and hobbled away, swearing to p. 68 have vengeance. Nasshut journeyed on and on, and at last arrived at the river Tuoni, which separates the land of the dead from the land of the living. There he waited until Lemminkainen should come, for he knew, by his wizard's skill, that he would come thither soon.

LEMMINKAINEN'S SECOND WOOING

FTER this Lemminkainen travelled on through dismal Pohjola until he came to the home of aged Louhi. He went in to Louhi and begged her to give him one of her daughters in marriage, but Louhi refused, saying: 'Thou hast already taken one wife from Lapland, the fair Kyllikki, and I will give thee neither the loveliest nor yet the ugliest of my daughters.'

Still Lemminkainen kept urging her, and at last, to get rid of him, she said: 'I will never give one of my daughters to a worthless man. Thou mayst not ask me again until thou bringest me the Hisi-reindeer.'

Then Lemminkainen set to work to make his arrows and his darts. When these were done he went to Lylikki, the great snow-shoe maker, and bade him make a huge p. 70 pair of snow-shoes, as he was going to hunt the Hisi-reindeer. At first Lylikki tried to dissuade him, telling him he could never succeed, but perhaps would die in the forest. But Lemminkainen ordered him again to make the snow-shoes, and Lylikki set to work. He made them of wood, only a few inches wide, but longer than Lemminkainen was tall, and with straps in the middle to fasten them on to the feet; and he also made a staff for Lemminkainen to push himself along with, or to keep his balance with when he slid down the hills.

At length they were finished, and Lemminkainen put them on, and his quiver on his back, and took his snow-staff in his hand, and as he set off he cried out: 'There is no living thing in all the forest that can escape me now, when I take my mighty strides in Lylikki's snow-shoes.'

But the evil spirit Hisi overheard him as he boasted thus, and Hisi set to work to make an enchanted reindeer, that Lemminkainen would never be able to catch. So he took bare willow branches to make the horns, and wood for the head, the feet and legs were made of reeds, and the veins from withered grass, the eyes were made from daisies, the ears from flowers, and the skin of the rough fir-bark, and the muscles from strong, sappy wood. When this magic reindeer was completed it was the swiftest and the p. 71 finest-looking of all reindeer. And Hisi sent it off to Pohjola, telling it to lure Lemminkainen into the snow-covered mountains and there to wear him out with the cold and the fatigue of the chase. So the reindeer went forth to dismal Pohjola, and there it ran through the courtyards and the outhouses, overturning tubs of water, throwing the kettles from their hooks, and upsetting the dishes that were cooking before the fires. There was a frightful noise there, for all the dogs began to bark, and the children to cry, and the women to laugh, and the men to shout. And then the magic reindeer went on its way.

Now Lemminkainen had set out, as soon as his snow-shoes were ready, and had hunted the whole world over for a trace of the Hisi-reindeer, rushing like the wind over mountains and valleys, until the fire shot from his snow-shoes, and his snow-staff smoked. But after he had wandered over the whole world and still had found no trace of the Hisi-reindeer, he came at last to the corner of Northland where the magic animal had just run through the courts upsetting everything, and the children were still crying and the women laughing when he arrived. Lemminkainen asked what the cause was of their uproar, and they told him how the reindeer had been there.

No sooner had he heard this than off he p. 72 flew over the snow, and as he went he sang a spell, calling on the powers of Pohjola to enable him to catch the Hisi-beast. After he had sung, he gave three huge strides with his snow-shoes, and at the end of the third he caught up with the Hisi-reindeer, and in another moment had it bound fast. Then he spoke to the reindeer and patted it on the head, and bade it come with him to Louhi. But suddenly the animal made a mighty rush, snapped his bonds in two, and sprang away over the hills and valleys out of sight.

Lemminkainen started off after it, but at the first step his snow-shoes broke right in two and threw him down, breaking his arrows and his snow-staff in his fall. Then he arose and looked sadly at his broken shoes and arrows and stick, and said to himself: 'How shall I ever succeed in my hunt, now that my shoes are broken, and the reindeer is once more free?'

LEMMINKAINEN'S DEATH

FOR a long time Lemminkainen sat considering whether he should give up the chase and return to Kalevala, or still keep on after the Hisi-reindeer. At length he regained hope and courage, and having sung an incantation that made his snow-shoes and arrows and staff whole again, he started off once more.

This time he turned his steps to the home of Tapio, the god of the forest, and as he went he began to sing wondrous songs to Tapio and his wife Mielikki, begging them to help him, and promising them great stores of gold and silver if they would do so.

At last he arrived at Tapio's palace, which had window-frames of gold, and the palace itself was of ivory. And within it Mielikki and her daughters were dressed in p. 74 golden garments, and wore gold and gems in their hair, and pearls round their necks. And they all promised to help Lemminkainen, and went off to drive the reindeer up to the palace so that he might catch it. Nor had he long to wait before whole troops of reindeer came flocking into the palace courtyard, and Lemminkainen saw among them the Hisi-deer, and caught it.

Then Lemminkainen sang a song of triumph, and having paid to Tapio's wife, Mielikki, the gold and silver he had promised, he hastened off with the reindeer to Louhi's home. But when he gave the Hisi-deer to her, she said: 'I will give thee my fairest daughter if thou wilt catch and bridle for me the fiery Hisi-horse, that breathes smoke and fire from his mouth and nostrils.'

So Lemminkainen went off, taking with him a golden bridle to put on the horse. For three days he wandered without catching sight of the Hisi-horse, but on the third day he climbed to the top of a very high mountain, and from thence he spied the steed on the plain amongst the fir-trees, breathing smoke and flames from his mouth and nostrils and eyes.

When Lemminkainen saw him he prayed to great Ukko to send a shower of icy hail upon the fiery Hisi-steed, and presently a great shower of hail rained down, and every hailstone was larger than a man's head. p. 75 After the hail was over, Lemminkainen came up to the fiery horse and coaxed him to let the golden bridle be slipped over his head. Then off they went like the wind, the horse obeying Lemminkainen perfectly, and in a very short time they arrived at Louhi's house. When he had given the Hisi-horse to Louhi, Lemminkainen asked again for the hand of her fairest daughter. But Louhi told him she would not give him her daughter until he had killed the swan that swam on Tuoni's river, which flows between the land of the living and the dead.

Then Lemminkainen started off fearlessly to seek the graceful swan of Tuoni, and journeyed on and on until at length he came to the coal-black river. There the old shepherd of Pohjola, Nasshut, was waiting for him, and, though blind, he heard Lemminkainen's footsteps, and sent a serpent from the death-river to meet him. The serpent stung Lemminkainen just over the heart, so that he fell down dead almost instantly, only having time to call upon his ancient mother to help him.

And Nasshut cast his body into the dismal river Tuoni, where it was washed down through the rapids to the Deathland, Tuonela. There the son of the ruler of the Deathland took the body, and cutting it into five portions, cast them back into the stream, saying: 'Swim there now, O Lemminkainen! p. 76 float for ever in this river, so that thou mayst hunt the wild swan at thy leisure.'

And thus the handsome Lemminkainen died, and was cast into the river of Tuoni, that flows along the Deathland.

LEMMINKAINEN'S RESTORATION

LEMMINKAINEN'S mother began to grow uneasy at his long absence, and to fear that some trouble had befallen him. At last one day, as his wife, the fair Kyllikki, was in her room, she noticed that drops of blood had begun to flow from the bristles of Lemminkainen's hair-brush. Then she began to weep and mourn, and ran and told his mother, who came and saw the blood oozing from the brush, and cried out:

'Woe is me, for my son, my hero, is in some terrible distress; some awful misfortune has happened to him.' Saying this she hurried off, and went straight to Louhi's house. There she asked what had become of her son, but Louhi only replied that she did not know, that he had driven off long ago in a sledge she had given him, p. 78 and perhaps the wolves or bears had eaten him.

'Thou art only telling falsehoods,' replied Lemminkainen's mother, 'for no bears or wolves can devour him; he would put them to sleep with his magic singing. Now, tell me truly, O Louhi, whither thou hast sent my son, or I will destroy all thy storehouses and even thy magic Sampo.'

And then Louhi said that she had given him a copper boat, and he had floated off on the river; perhaps he had perished in the rapids below. But Lemminkainen's mother answered: 'Thou art still speaking falsely. Tell me the truth this time, or I will send plague and death upon thee.'

Then Louhi answered the third time: 'I will tell thee the truth. I sent him to fetch me the Hisi-reindeer, and then after the fire-breathing horse, and last of all, after the swan that swims the death-stream, Tuoni, that he might gain the hand of my fairest daughter. He may have perished there, for he has not come back since to ask for my daughter's hand.'

No sooner had Louhi said this than the anxious mother hurried off to hunt for her son. Over hills and valleys, through marsh and forest, and over the wide waters she went, but looked for him in vain. Then she asked the Trees if they had seen him but they answered: 'We have more than p. 79 enough to think of with our own griefs. We are cut down with cruel axes and burned to death, and no one pities us.'

So she wandered on and on, and finally she asked the Paths if they had seen her son pass by. But the Paths replied: 'Our own lives are too wretched to think of other people's sorrows. We are trodden under foot by beasts and men, and the heavy carts cut us in pieces.'

Next she asked the Moon, but the Moon replied: 'I have trouble enough of my own. I have to wander all alone in both summer and winter nights, and have no rest.'

Next she questioned the Sun, and he was kinder than the rest, and told her how her son had died in the gloomy river Tuoni.

Then she hastened to Ilmarinen, the wondrous smith, and bade him make a huge rake for her out of copper, with teeth a hundred fathoms long and the handle five hundred fathoms. Ilmarinen quickly forged a magic rake, and she hurried off with it to the gloomy river Tuoni, praying as she went: 'O Sun, whom Ukko hath created, shine for me now with magic power into the kingdom of death, into dark Manala, and lull all the evil spirits there to sleep.'

The Sun came and sat upon a birch-tree near the river of Tuoni, and shone upon the Deathland, Tuonela, until all the spirits fell asleep. Then he rose, and hovering over p. 80 them, warmed them into a yet deeper slumber, and then hurried back to his place in the sky.

Meanwhile Lemminkainen's mother had raked a long time in the coal-black river, but could find nothing. Then she waded in deeper and deeper, until she could reach into the deepest caverns with her rake. First, she found his jacket, and then the rest of his clothing; and finally, the third time she swept her rake along, it brought up Lemminkainen's body, but the hands and arms and head were still missing. Still she went on with her search, and at length all the pieces were gathered together.

When she had laid them beside each other, in their proper positions, she began to pray to the goddess of the veins, Suonetar, and the maiden of the ether, to come and join the different parts together, and to sew up the wounds and make him whole. And then she prayed to the mighty Ukko to help them, and to heal every part that was wounded or bruised, to touch them with his magic touch, and restore Lemminkainen to life.

And Ukko did so, and Lemminkainen lived once more, but he was still blind and deaf and dumb. But his mother considered deeply how she might restore these senses to him, and at length she called the little bee to her, and bade it go out and p. 81 collect honey from the healing plants in the meadows. So the bee flew away and returned very soon laden with honey from all the healing plants, and she anointed her son with this, but it only gave him his sight, and still left him deaf and dumb.

Again the mother sent off the bee, telling it to go across the seven oceans, and to alight on an enchanted isle in the eighth. There it would find magic honey to bring back. The bee did as it was told and found the magic honey-balm in tiny earthen vessels, and flew back with seven vessels in its arms and seven on each shoulder, all filled with the magic honey-balm. Lemminkainen's mother anointed him with this, and he could hear, but still remained speechless.

Then the mother bade the bee fly up to the seventh heaven and to bring down from thence the honey of Ukko's wisdom, which was so abundant there. When the bee declared that it could not fly so high, she told it the way and sent it off. So the bee flew up and up, and at the end of the first day it rested on the moon. At the end of the second day it reached the shoulders of the Great Bear, and on the third day it flew over the Great Bear's head and reached the seventh heaven of Ukko. There it found three golden kettles, and in the first was a balm that gave ease to the heart, and p. 82 the balm in the second gave happiness, but the balm of the third kettle gave life. So the bee took some of the life-giving balm and hastened back to earth.

Then Lemminkainen's mother anointed him with this magic balm, speaking a magic spell as she rubbed him with it, and immediately he awoke, and his first words were: 'Truly I have been sleeping long, but yet my sleep was a sweet one, for I knew neither joy nor sorrow.'

When his mother asked how he had gone thither and who it was that had harmed him, he told her all — how Louhi had sent him for the swan, and how old Nasshut, the blind Northland shepherd, had sent the serpent against him and killed him, for he did not know the charm to cure the sting of serpents. Then his mother upbraided him for his ignorance, and told him how the serpent was born from the marrow of the duck and the brain of swallows, mixed with Suojatar's saliva, and she told him too what the spell was to use against them. Thus his mother brought him back to life and health, and he was wiser and handsomer than ever, but still he was downhearted.

His mother asked him the reason of this, and he replied that he was still thinking of Louhi's daughter and longing for her as his bride, but that first he must shoot the wild p. 83 swan. But his mother answered: 'Do not think of the wild swan, nor yet of Louhi's daughters. Return with me to Kalevala to thy home, and thank and praise thy Maker, Ukko, that he hath saved thee, for I alone could never have saved thee from dismal Manala.'

So Lemminkainen hastened home with his mother, — back again to his pleasant home in Kalevala.

Every one expressed satisfaction that Lemminkainen had been restored to life — 'for, you see,' said Mimi, 'though he was really a bad man, he did so many wonderful things that you just can't help wishing for him not to be killed.'

But now it had grown quite late, nearly nine o'clock, and so they all ate their supper and then Erik and Father Mikko sat smoking and talking while Mother Stina and the little ones went into the other room to bed, — for Erik had actually two rooms in his house, — and it isn't every Finnish country cabin that has that, you know. They talked of their country, for that was the dearest subject to both of them, — they were intelligent men for their class, — and when Father Mikko told how the Russian Tsar was taking their liberties away from them, and was beginning to break all p. 84 his oaths and promises and would no doubt end up by making them as badly off as the people on the south side of the Finnish Gulf — when Father

Mikko related all this, Erik's eyes flashed and he longed to be able to draw the sword to defend his beloved country's liberty.

But at last they had gone over all these things and were sleepy themselves, so they made up their beds on some sheep-skin rugs on the floor, and soon fell into a sound sleep.

The next day it was still storming, and so Father Mikko gave up all idea of leaving that day. About three o'clock in the afternoon—it was dark as night then—they had all finished dinner and settled down around the fire as on the day before, and Father Mikko was easily persuaded to go on with his stories.

Erik was at work on a pair of snow-shoes, just like those that Lemminkainen wore in the story of the hunt after the Hisi-deer. They were nearly finished—about six feet long and five inches wide in the broadest part, with a place in the middle to fasten them on to the feet, and the front ends were turned up. All that now remained to be done was to polish them off, and Erik worked at this while Father Mikko told his p. 85 stories. The children had enough to do to watch 'Pappa' Mikko's face and listen to the wonderful tales, and Mother Stina was busy with some sewing—she couldn't spin because the noise of the wheel would have drowned Father Mikko's voice.

'Now that we have brought Lemminkainen back from the Death-river,' the old man said, 'we will see what Wainamoinen was doing all this while.' So he began as follows:

WAINAMOINEN'S BOAT-BUILDING

WAINAMOINEN started to build a boat from the Rainbow-maiden's distaff, but he had soon used up all his timber, and the boat was far from finished. So he asked Sampsa (the planter of the first trees that grew on earth) to go and search out the needful timber in order to finish the boat.

Sampsa started off with a golden axe upon his shoulder and a copper hatchet in his belt. He wandered through the mountain forests, and at length came upon a great aspen, and was just going to cut it down, when the aspen asked him what he wanted. 'I wish to take your timber for a vessel,' Sampsa replied, 'that the wise magician Wainamoinen is building.' Then the aspen answered: 'All the boats that have been made of my wood have been p. 87 but failures; they float but a little way, and then sink to the ocean's bottom, for my trunk is full of hollow places, where the worms have eaten my wood.'

So Sampsa left the aspen and searched still further, until he came to a pine-tree that was even taller than the aspen was. Sampsa struck a blow with his axe, and at the same time asked the pine-tree if it would furnish good timber for Wainamoinen's boat. But the pine-tree answered: 'All the ships that have been made from me are useless. I am full of imperfections, for the ravens live among my branches and bring ill-luck.'

And Sampsa was obliged to leave the pine-tree and go on until he came to a tremendous oak-tree, whose trunk was thicker than the height of even the tallest men. And he asked the oak-tree if it would furnish wood for Wainamoinen's boat. 'I will gladly furnish the wood,' replied the oak-tree, 'for I am tall and sound and strong. The warm sun shines upon me for three months in the summer, and the sacred cuckoo dwells in my branches and brings good fortune.' So

Sampsa quickly felled the oak, and brought the timber, skilfully hewn, to Wainamoinen.

The wise magician Wainamoinen then began to put his boat together by the aid of magic spells. The first magic song that p. 88 he sang joined the framework together, and the second song fastened the planking into the ribs, and the third put the rowlocks in place and made the oars. But, alas! when all this was done, there were still three magic words needed to complete the stem and stern and bulwarks.

Wainamoinen saw that all his labour was in vain unless he found the three magic words, for unless the stern and stem were fastened and the bulwarks built, the boat could never put to sea. He pondered long over where he might find the lost words, and after a while he concluded that they might be found in the brains of swallows and the heads of swans and the plumage of the sea-duck. But though he killed great numbers of these birds, he could not find the three lost words. Then he thought that he might find them on the tongues of reindeers or of the squirrels; but though he killed great numbers of them, and found many words on their tongues, the three lost words were not there.

Then he said to himself: 'I will seek the lost words in the kingdom of Manala; there are countless words to be found there in the Deathland.' So off he went, travelling for three weeks over hill and dale, through marshes and thickets, until at length he came to the river of Tuoni. There he called out in a voice like thunder: 'Bring a boat, p. 89 O daughter of Tuoni, and ferry me over this black and fatal river.'

Tuoni's daughter, a wee little dwarf, but very wise and ancient, bade him first say why he wished to come into the Deathland while he was still alive. And first Wainamoinen answered that Tuoni himself, the death-god, had sent him. But the maid replied: 'Had Tuoni brought thee, he would now be with thee, and thou wouldst be wearing his cap and gloves.' So Wainamoinen answered again: 'I was slain by an iron weapon.' But the maid would not believe him, because he had no bleeding wound. Then he said the third time, that he had been washed there by the river. But still the maid would not believe him, for his clothing was not wet. And the fourth time he said that fire had burnt him. But the maid replied: 'If the fire had brought thee to Manala, thy hair and eyebrows and beard would be all singed and burnt. But now I ask thee for the last time what it is that hath brought thee, living, hither. Tell me the truth this time.'

Then Wainamoinen told her that he had been building a boat by magic, but that he yet lacked one spell, and had come thither to seek it. When he had said this, Tuoni's daughter came across and rowed him to the opposite side, having first tried to dissuade him from coming. But Wainamoinen was p. 90 not afraid; and when he had landed he walked straight up to the abode of Tuoni.

There Tuonetar, Tuoni's wife, gave him a golden goblet filled with beer, saying: 'Drink Tuoni's beer, O wise and ancient Wainamoinen!' But he carefully inspected the liquor before he tasted it, and saw that it was black and full of the spawn of frogs and poisonous serpent-broods; and he said to Tuonetar: 'I have not come hither to drink Tuoni's poisons, for they that do so will surely be destroyed.'

Tuonetar then asked him why he had come, and he told her of his boat-building, and how he still needed the three magic words, and that he hoped to find them there. 'Tuoni will never reveal them,' Tuonetar said; 'nor shalt thou ever leave these gates alive;' and as she spoke she waved the slumber-wand over Wainamoinen's head, and he sank into a deep sleep. And to make sure of his not escaping, Tuoni's son, a hideous wizard with only three fingers, wove nets of iron and of copper, and set them all through the river, to catch Wainamoinen if by any chance he should get so far.

But Wainamoinen soon freed himself from Tuonetar's slumber-spell, and knowing in how great danger he was, he instantly transformed himself into a serpent, and wriggled his way to the river, and through p. 91 the nets that had been set to catch him, until at length he came out safe into the land of the living again; and the next morning, when Tuoni's wizard son went to look at his nets, he found all kinds of evil fish and serpents, but not the wise old magician.

But Wainamoinen prayed to Ukko: 'I thank thee, O Ukko, that thou hast protected me; but never suffer any other of thy heroes, not even the wisest, to go against the laws of nature to the awful Tuonela. For there are but few who return from thence.'

And then Wainamoinen called together the people on the plains of Kalevala, and spoke to the young men and maidens, saying: 'Listen, all ye young people. Never disobey your parents; never harm the innocent, nor wrong the weak, nor utter falsehood, else ye will pay the penance for it in the gloomy prison of Manala; for there is the dwelling-place of the wicked, and a place for the guilty. Beneath the burning rocks there are fiery couches, with pillows of hissing serpents, and coverlets of green writhing vipers. And the wicked there drink the blood of adders, but have nothing to eat at all. If ye would be happy, shun this abode of the wicked ones in Tuonela.'

'But I thought Wainamoinen wasn't to p. 92 use any wood for his boat except the pieces of the distaff,' said Mimi.

'Well, you see,' said Father Mikko, 'the main thing was to build the boat by *magic*, and we'll see now how he did that. I don't believe a little extra wood made any difference.' So he went on:

A LAPLAND WIZARD.

WAINAMOINEN FINDS THE LOST WORDS

 WAINAMOINEN had failed to find the three magic words in the Deathland, and now he sat and pondered whither he should go next to seek them. While he was thinking over this, a shepherd came to him and said: 'Thou canst find a thousand words of wisdom on the tongue of the dead hero Wipunen. I know the road that leads to his grave: first, thou must journey a long distance over the points of needles, and then a long way upon the edges of sharp swords, and then a third road on the edges of hatchets.'

Then Wainamoinen considered how he should be able to walk over the needles and swords and hatchets, and at last hit on a plan. He went to the smith Ilmarinen and bade him make shoes of iron, and gloves of copper, and a magic staff of the p. 96 sent by mighty Ukko, for if so I will be resigned, but if thou art of some human race, I will search out thy tribe and destroy it. Leave my body, cease thy forging, let me rest in peace and slumber. Or if thou wilt not leave me, I will call on all the great magicians of the past, the spirits of the mountains and woods and seas and rivers, on Ilmatar, daughter of the ether, to assist me. Or if these be not sufficient, I will call on mighty Ukko to drive thee forth. If thou art from the winds, then return to the copper mountains where they live; if from the sea, return to it; if from the forests, then return to them, or I will drive thee to the bottom of the coal-black river of Tuoni, whence thou shalt never move again.'

'I am well contented here,' said Wainamoinen, 'in these roomy caverns. I can eat thy heart and flesh and for drink I will take thy blood. And I will set my forge still deeper in thy vitals, and will swing my hammer still harder on thy heart and lungs and liver. I shall never leave thee until I learn all thy wisdom, and the three lost words, that all thy magic knowledge may not perish with thee from the earth.'

Then Wipunen began to sing all his knowledge and his magic spells for Wainamoinen. He sang the origin of witchcraft, the source of good and evil and p. 97 how by the will of Ukko the water was first divided from the ether. And next he sang of how the moon and sun were made, and whence the colours of the rainbow came, and how the stars were sprinkled in the sky. Three whole days and nights he sang, until the stars and the moon stood still to listen, and the very waves of the sea and the tides ceased to rise and fall, and the rivers stopped in their courses.

At length Wainamoinen had learned all the wisdom of the great magician, and the three lost words, and he made ready to leave Wipunen's body, bidding him open wide his mouth that he might get out and leave him for ever.

'I have eaten many things, O Wainamoinen,' said Wipunen, 'bears and reindeer, wolves and oxen, but never such a thing as thou. Now thou hast found the wisdom that thou seekest, go in peace and never come back to me.'

Then he opened his mouth wide, and Wainamoinen glided forth and hastened swiftly as the deer to Kalevala. First he went into the smithy, and Ilmarinen asked him if he had learned the lost words that would enable him to finish his vessel. 'I have learned a thousand magic words,' answered Wainamoinen, 'and among them are the lost words that I sought.'

Thereupon he hastened off to where his p. 98 vessel lay, and with the three lost words he joined the stem and stern and raised the bulwarks. Thus he had built the vessel with magic alone, and by magic art he launched it too, not touching it with foot or knee or hand, using only magic to push it. Thus was the task completed which should gain for him the Rainbow-maiden in her beauty.

'Oh! *do* hurry and tell us about that,' said Mimi, and Father Mikko continued.

THE RIVAL SUITORS

NOW the Rainbow-maiden was really the same as old Louhi's fairest daughter, whom Wainamoinen had wooed, and for whom Ilmarinen had made the magic Sampo, and Wainamoinen had learned this. So when the magic boat was finished, he made ready for a journey to the Northland, to try once more to win the fair Pohjola maiden for his bride.

He ornamented the magic vessel with gold and silver, and painted it scarlet, and on the masts he set sails of linen, red, white, and blue. Then he stepped on board, and called on Ukko to protect and help him, and on the winds to aid him on his way, and off the magic boat flew towards Pohjola, never needing an oar to help it.

Annikki, Ilmarinen's sister, was down by the seashore just at dawn that morning, p. 100 and as she gazed out over the sea, she saw a blue speck in the distance. At first she thought it was a flock of birds, and then as it drew nearer it looked like a great tree floating on the water, but at last she saw that it was a vessel with but one man in it, and when it came still nearer she recognised Wainamoinen.

She called out to him and asked him whither he was going. He replied that he was come a-fishing, but Annikki said: 'Thy boat is not rigged like a fisher-boat, nor hast thou lines or nets with thee. Tell me the truth, O Wainamoinen!' And he answered the second time, that he had come to kill wild geese and ducks. But Annikki told him that she knew that was untrue, for he had no hunting dogs in the vessel with him, nor any weapons. Then he told her that he was sailing to the wars. Annikki replied: 'My father often used to sail to war, but in a ship with many rowers, and with many armed heroes on board, but thy vessel is surely not fitted for battle. Now tell me the truth, O wise Wainamoinen, or else I will send a storm-wind after thee and break thy ship in pieces.'

Then he told her the truth, that he was going to woo the Rainbow-maiden, Louhi's daughter, and then Annikki knew that he spoke the truth. She hurried off to her brother's smithy and said to him: 'Dearest p. 101 brother, if thou wilt forge for me a silver loom and gold and silver finger-rings and earrings, golden girdles and golden ornaments for my hair, I will tell thee something that is very important for thee to know.'

So Ilmarinen promised, and his sister said: 'O Ilmarinen, if thou hopest ever to wed the fair maid of Pohjola, thou must hasten and make thy sledge ready, for Wainamoinen is now sailing thither in a magic boat to win her before thee.' Then Ilmarinen bade his sister prepare a magic soap and make a bath ready for him while he was forging the gold and silver ornaments that she had bargained for.

When Ilmarinen had finished his work he found the bath and the magic soap all ready for him, and he began to wash off the grime and dirt and soot of the smithy. When he was through, and came out of the bath, he had grown wonderfully bright and handsome, for the magic soap had made his cheeks rosy and his eyes bright as moonlight. Then he put on his finest garments, soft linen, and silken stockings, a blue vest and scarlet trousers, and a fur coat of sealskin, held by buttons made of jewels, and a belt with golden buckles. After he was dressed he ordered his magic sledge to be harnessed, and on the front placed six cuckoos and seven blue-birds that they might sing and charm the Northland maiden. p. 102

When all was ready Ilmarinen prayed to great Ukko to send snow that it might cover all the country and let his sledge glide easily to Pohjola. And the snow came, and Ilmarinen wrapped himself up warmly in bear-skins, and drove off like the wind, first invoking Ukko's blessing on his journey. On he went, over hill and dale, with the cuckoos and blue-birds singing on the sledge, and then he drove along the seashore to the north in a cloud of snow and sand and mist and sea-foam, looking out for Wainamoinen's vessel. On the evening of the third day he caught up with Wainamoinen, and called out to him: 'O ancient Wainamoinen, let us woo the maiden peacefully, and let her choose which one of us she will.' To this Wainamoinen agreed; and having promised not to use deceit of any sort against one another, they hurried on their way,—Wainamoinen calling up the south wind to help him, and Ilmarinen's steed shaking the hills of Northland as he galloped on.

Soon they drew near to Louhi's dwelling, and the watchdogs began to bark more loudly than they had ever done before. Louhi's husband told his daughter to go and see what the trouble was, but she replied that she was busy grinding barley, and could not go. Then he told his wife to go, but she was too busy cooking dinner. So the p. 103 father grew angry, and said: 'Women are always busy either baking or sleeping; go, my son, and learn what all the trouble is.' But the son refused, because he was busy splitting wood.

So at last Louhi's husband was obliged to go himself, for the dogs kept barking louder and louder. There, as soon as he had reached the gate, he saw a scarlet-coloured ship sailing into the bay, and a sledge driving up along the shore at full speed. Then he hastened back into the house, and told them all that he had seen. And Louhi took a branch and gave it to her daughter, saying: 'Place this on the fire, my daughter, and if in burning it drips blood, then these strangers bring war and bloodshed; but if clear water, then they come in peace.'

So the maiden put the branch on the fire, and as they watched it they saw honey trickling out, and from this Louhi knew that the two men were coming as suitors. Then they hastened out into the courtyard, and saw the vessel in the harbour, painted scarlet, and an ancient white-bearded magician at the helm; and on the land they saw a brightly-coloured sledge, with cuckoos and bluebirds singing on the front, and driven by a young and handsome hero.

Louhi immediately recognised them both, and said to her daughter: 'Wilt thou have p. 104 one of these suitors, dearest daughter? He that comes in the ship is good old Wainamoinen, bringing countless treasures for thee from Kalevala. The other in the sledge, with the singing birds, is the blacksmith Ilmarinen, who brings no presents save himself. When they come into the house bring a pitcher of honey-drink, and give it to the one that thou wilt follow. Give it to old Wainamoinen, for he brings thee countless treasures.'

But the daughter replied: 'I will never marry a man for riches, but for his real worth. Mothers did not use to sell their daughters thus in the olden times to suitors whom they did not love. I shall choose Ilmarinen for his true worth and wisdom.'

Old Louhi grew angry at this, and tried to change her daughter's mind, but all she could say did not move her; and just then Wainamoinen came to the house, and addressed the maiden thus: 'Come with me, O lovely maiden, be my bride and honoured wife, and share my joys and sorrows with me.'

The maiden answered: 'Hast thou built the magic vessel, using neither hand nor foot to touch it?'

'I have built it, and brought it hither,' answered Wainamoinen. 'It is finely made by magic, and will live in the worst of storms; nothing can ever sink it.' p. 105

But then the maiden said to him: 'I will not wed a husband born in the sea. Storms would bring us trouble, and the winds rack our hearts. I cannot go with thee, cannot marry thee, O Wainamoinen.'

ILMARINEN'S WOOING

 JUST as Wainamoinen had received his answer, Ilmarinen came hurrying into the house and into the guest-room. There servants brought him honey-drink in silver pitchers, but he said: 'I will never taste the drink of Northland till I see the Rainbow-maiden. With her I will gladly drink, for I have come hither to seek her hand.' Then Louhi said to him: 'The maiden is not ready to receive thee, and thou may not woo her before thou hast ploughed the field of hissing serpents. Once the evil spirit Lempo ploughed it, but it has never been done since.'

Ilmarinen wandered off sadly, but while he was pondering over what he should do, he saw the lovely maid herself. He went up to her and said: 'Long ago I forged the Sampo for thee, and then thou promised to p. 107 become my wife. But now thy mother demands that I first plough the field of serpents before I win thee.' But the maiden comforted him, and told him how to plough the field with a plough of gold and silver and copper.

So Ilmarinen went off and built a smithy, and placed in the furnace gold and silver and copper and iron. And from these he forged a plough, with ploughshare of gold and beam of silver and copper handles; and for himself he made boots and gloves and armour of iron; and as he worked he sang magic spells to give his work power to overcome the serpents. Then he harnessed to the plough the fire-breathing Hisi-horse, and went into the field. There were serpents of every sort, creeping and crawling over one another, and hissing horribly, but Ilmarinen cast a spell over them, and ploughed the field, so that all the snakes were buried in the furrows. And then he went to Louhi, and claimed her daughter's hand.

But Louhi refused to let him have her daughter until he should catch the great bear of Manala, and bring him to her. So he went off to the maid again, and told her what old Louhi had demanded of him. The lovely maiden instructed him how to prepare a muzzle for the bear, forging it of steel on a rock beneath the water, at a spot where p. 108 three currents met together, and the straps were to be of steel and copper mixed. And Ilmarinen made a muzzle as she had directed, and set off for Manala, the dismal Deathland. As he went he prayed to the goddess of the mists to send a fog where the great bear of Manala was, so that he might not see Ilmarinen as he approached. And the goddess sent the fog, and Ilmarinen was able to creep up to the bear and throw the magic muzzle over his head, and then to lead him to Louhi without any trouble.

When he had brought the bear to her, he asked her again for her lovely daughter's hand. But Louhi said to him: 'Thou must perform one more task still, and then, when that is done, thou shalt have my dear daughter. Catch for me the monster-pike that lives in the river of Tuoni, but thou may not use hook, nor line, nor nets, nor boat. Hundreds have been sent to catch it, but all have died in Tuoni's dark waters.'

And now Ilmarinen was deeply discouraged, and went off to tell the maiden of this third task, which he thought it was impossible to do. But she told him to forge an eagle in his magic furnace, and that the eagle would catch the monster-pike for him. So Ilmarinen went to work and forged an eagle in his smithy: talons of iron, beak of steel and copper. And when the eagle was entirely made from iron and copper, he p. 109 mounted on its back and bade it fly away to the river of Tuoni, there to catch the monster-pike. When they had reached the bank, Ilmarinen dismounted and began to search for the pike, while the eagle hovered over the water. While Ilmarinen was searching, a huge monster rose from the depths and tried to seize him, but the eagle swooped down, and with one bite of his mighty beak, wrenched off the monster's head. Still Ilmarinen continued his search, until at last the monster-pike itself rose up to seize him. But as it came to the surface, the giant-eagle swooped down upon it, and buried its talons in the pike's flesh. Then the fish, maddened with the pain, rushed down to the deepest caverns, dragging the eagle with it until the bird had to loose its hold and soar aloft again. A second time the eagle swooped down and struck deep into the pike's shoulders; but the pike dived to the bottom again and escaped. At last the eagle made a third descent, and this time grasped the pike firmly with his beak of steel, and planted his talons firmly on the rocks, and this time he succeeded in dragging the pike from out the river.

Then the eagle flew off with the pike to the top of a tall pine-tree, and there ate the body of his victim, leaving the head for Ilmarinen. But the eagle himself soared up into the air, up beyond the clouds, p. 110 and at length disappeared behind the sun.

Ilmarinen returned to Louhi with the pike's head and again claimed her daughter in marriage. Louhi answered him: 'Thou hast performed this last task but badly, since thou only brought me the worthless head. But still, since thou hast completed the other tasks also, I will give thee my fair daughter. Thou hast won the Maid of Beauty, to be the help and joy of all thy future life.'

But while Ilmarinen was rejoicing in his good fortune, the aged Wainamoinen wandered sorrowfully homewards, bewailing his sad lot, thus to be compelled to live without a wife to cheer his home. 'Woe is me,' he sang, 'that I did not woo and marry in my youth, for the old men cannot hope to conquer the young ones when they go a-wooing.'

When this story was ended, Father Mikko stopped a while to rest, and the others discussed the stories that he had just told. All were pleased that the Rainbow-maiden had chosen Ilmarinen instead of the aged Wainamoinen, and little Antero asked 'Pappa' Mikko what they had had to eat at the wedding—he was rather more deeply interested in things to eat than anything else—so Father Mikko continued, after he had rested a while.

THE BREWING OF BEER

GREAT preparations were now made in Louhi's home for her daughter's wedding with Ilmarinen. In distant Karjala, a part of Kalevala, was a great ox, the largest in the world. It took a weasel seven days to travel round his neck and shoulders; the swallow had to fly a whole day without resting, to get from one horn-tip to the other; the squirrel travelled thirty days, starting from the tail, before he reached the shoulders. This great ox was led by a thousand heroes to Pohjola, to Louhi's house, but when he had come thither, no one could be found to kill him.

Then there came an aged hero from Karjala, and went up to the ox to kill him with his war-club. But the ox turned and gave him one fierce glance, and the old warrior dropped his club and ran away and p. 112 hid in the forest. Then they sent forth far and near to find some one to kill the ox, but no one came. At last there arose from the sea a tiny dwarf, who, when he stepped on land, grew suddenly into a giant, with hands of iron, a copper-coloured face, a hat of flint upon his head, and sandstone shoes upon his feet. As soon as this sea-spirit saw the ox, he rushed at it and killed it with one blow of his golden sword. Thus was the meat provided for the feast.

The banquet-hall was so large that when a dog barked at one door no one could hear him at the opposite side, and when a cock crowed on the roof no one on the ground could hear him. Louhi went in thither, to see that all was being put in readiness, but while she was there she said aloud as if to herself: 'Whence will I get the liquor for my guests, for I know nothing of the secret of beer-brewing?'

An old man was sitting beside the fire, and he answered her: 'Beer comes from barley, hops, and water. The seed of the hops were scattered loosely over the earth, and from them arose the graceful hop-vine, climbing over everything. The barley was planted in the land of Kalevala, and it grew and flourished there.

'Then the hops, clinging to the trees, began to hum, and the barley and the water in the wells to sing, saying: "Let us join p. 113 our forces together, that we may live united, for that is far better than to be separated as we now are." So the ancient maiden Osmotar took six golden grains of barley, seven hops, and seven cups of water, and set them in a caldron on the fire. There she let them steep and boil during the warm summer days, and at length poured off the liquor into tubs made of birch-wood. Now she pondered long how she should make the liquor ferment and cause it to foam and sparkle.

'Then Osmotar called one of the Kalevala maidens and bade her step into the birchen tub. The maiden did so, and on looking around she saw a splinter of wood lying on the bottom. She picked it up, thinking it was worthless, but nevertheless she took it to Osmotar. Osmotar rubbed her hands upon her knees and turned the bit of wood into a white squirrel. As soon as she had made the squirrel, she sent it off to Tapio's kingdom, to the great forest, and commanded it to bring her cones from the magic fir-trees and young shoots from the magic pines. And the squirrel hurried off and travelled through the forest until it came to Tapio's home. There it found three magic pine-trees growing, and three fir-trees beside them, and having taken the young shoots and the cones and stowed them in its pouch, it came back again to p. 114 Osmotar. But when she put the cones and pine-shoots into the beer, it still refused to ferment.

'So Osmotar made the Kalevala maiden get into the birchen tub once more, and this time the maiden found a chip upon the bottom. When she took it to Osmotar, the latter rubbed her hands upon her knees again, and turned the chip into a magic golden-breasted marten. Then she sent the marten off to the dens of the mountain bears, to gather the foam from their angry lips as they fought with one another. The marten flew away, and soon returned with the foam that it had gathered from the mouths of the raging bears. But when Osmotar added it to the liquor there was no effect, and the beer remained as still as ever.

'For a third time, then, the maid of Kalevala stepped into the tub, and this time found a pod on the bottom. Osmotar took the pod and rubbed it between her hands and knees, and there flew out of it a honeybee. She sent the bee off to the Islands of the Sea, telling it to go to a meadow there, where a maiden lay asleep, and growing by the maiden's side there were honey-grasses and fragrant flowers. From these the bee was to collect the honey and bring it back. The bee flew off straight over the ocean, and on the evening of the third day reached p. 115 the Isles of the Sea, where it found the maiden fast asleep amongst the flowers, clad in a silver robe, with a girdle of copper. By her grew the loveliest and sweetest of flowers and grasses, and the bee loaded itself down with their honey and returned to Osmotar with it. This time, when the honey was placed in the beer it began to ferment and rise and bubble and foam until it filled all the tubs and ran over on the sands.

'When the beer was ready, all the heroes of Kalevala came to drink it, and Lemminkainen drank so much that he became intoxicated. But Osmotar, now that she had made the beer, did not know how to keep it, for it was still running out of the tubs and over everything. While she was sitting and grieving over this, the robin sang to her from an aspen, and told her to put it into strong oaken barrels bound with copper hoops, and thus the last difficulty was overcome.

'Thus was beer first brewed from hops and barley,' continued the old man, 'and the beer of Kalevala is famed to strengthen the feeble, to cheer the sad, to make the old young, and the timid brave. It makes the heart joyful and puts wise sayings on the tongue, but the fool it makes still more foolish.'

Thus the old man ended his account of p. 116 the origin of beer, and Louhi, who had listened to him carefully, took all the tubs she had and put hops and barley in them, and water on top, and then lit huge fires to heat stones, that she might drop them in the mixture and make it boil. She made such a great quantity of beer that the springs were emptied and the forests grew small, and such a vast column of smoke went up as filled half of Pohjola and was seen even in distant Karjala and Lemminkainen's home. And all the people there thought it arose from some mighty battle between great heroes. But Lemminkainen pondered over it, and at last he found out that it was the fires for Louhi's beer-making for the wedding feast, and he grew bitterly angry, for Louhi had refused *him* her daughter's hand, and now had given her to Ilmarinen.

But now the beer was ready and was stored away in casks hooped with copper, and thousands of delicate dishes were made ready for the feast. But when all was nearly ready the beer began to grow impatient in its casks, and cried out for the guests to come that songs might be sung in its honour. So Louhi sent first for a pike and a salmon to sing its praises, but they could not do it. Next she sent for a boy, but the boy was too ignorant to sing the praises of the beer, and all this time the p. 117 beer was calling out more and more loudly from its prison. Then Louhi determined to invite the guests at once, lest the beer should break forth from the casks.

So she called one of her servants and said to her: 'Go, my trusted servant, and call together all the Pohjola people to the banquet. Go out into the highways too, and bring in all the poor and blind and cripples, the old and the young, that they may be merry at my daughter's wedding. And ask all the people of Karjala and the ancient Wainamoinen, but be sure thou dost not invite wild Lemminkainen.' At this the servant asked why she was not to ask Lemminkainen, and Louhi answered: 'Lemminkainen must not come, for he loves war and strife, and would bring disturbance and sorrow to our feast, and scoff at our maidens.'

And the servant, having learned from Louhi how she should recognise Lemminkainen, set off and invited rich and poor, old and young, the deaf, the blind, and the cripples in all Pohjola and Karjala, but did not ask Lemminkainen.

ILMARINEN'S WEDDING FEAST

 AT length the guests began to arrive, and Ilmarinen came escorted by hundreds of his friends, driving a coal-black steed, and with the same birds singing on his sledge as when he came to woo the Rainbow-maiden, Louhi's fairest daughter. When he alighted from his sledge, Louhi sent her best servants to take the steed and give him the very best of food in a manger of pure gold. But as Ilmarinen advanced to enter the house, they found that he was too tall to pass through the doorway without stooping, which would have been very unlucky: so Louhi had to have the top beam taken away before he could enter.

Inside the dwelling was so changed that no one would have recognised it. Louhi had cast a magic spell over it, and all the beams and door and window-sills were made p. 119 from bones that gleamed like ivory; the windows were adorned with trout-scales, and the fires were set in flowers; and the seats and tables and floors were of gold and silver and copper, with marble hearth-stones and silken carpets on the floors. Louhi bade Ilmarinen welcome when he came into the guest-hall, and calling up her servant-maidens, she gazed at her daughter's suitor. The maidens bore wax tapers, and by their light the bridegroom looked handsomer than ever, and his eyes sparkled like the waves of the sea.

LAPP WOMAN IN HOLIDAY COSTUME.

Then Louhi bade the maidens lead Ilmarinen to the seat of honour at the table in the great hall, and then all the other guests took their places, and the feast began. First of all the daintiest dishes of every sort were served by Louhi to the bridegroom—honey-biscuits, river-salmon, butter, bacon, and every delicacy one can think of—and after he was served, the servants took the dishes around to the others. After this the foaming beer was brought in silver pitchers, and all were served in the same order.

All the heroes and magicians assembled there began to grow merry, and Wainamoinen said that some one should sing the praises of the beer. But no one else could be found to do it, and all pressed Wainamoinen to sing, so at last he arose and be p. 120 gan. He sang of the beer first, and then from his great stock of wisdom he sang them one song after the other of the days of old, until every guest grew happy from his magic power of song. But when Wainamoinen had finished his singing, he added: 'Yet I am but a poor singer. For if great Ukko should sing his perfect songs of wisdom, he would sing the oceans into honey and the sands to berries, and the pebbles into barley, the rivers into beer, the fruit to gold, and the mountains into bread. Grant thy blessing, great Ukko, upon this feast of ours. Send joy and health and comfort to all those here, that we may ever look back with pleasure to Ilmarinen's marriage with the fair Maiden of the Rainbow.'

Thus Wainamoinen, the great singer, ended his singing, and the time had come for the bride and bridegroom to leave for their distant home in Kalevala. But first must Osmotar, the wise maiden, instruct the bride as to her future life. Osmotar told her that she must henceforth be thoughtful and not foolish, that she must love her husband's kinsfolks as her own. Osmotar told her, too, never to be idle, and then instructed her in all the many household duties of the wives of Kalevala, but at the same time impressed it upon her how wicked she would be if with all this she were to forget her own parents. After this Osmotar p. 121 turned to the bridegroom and bade him ever love his bride and honour her, nor ever treat her ill.

Thus she advised them both, and they made ready to leave. But the Maiden of the Rainbow wept, because she was leaving all the joys and pleasures of her youth, and those she loved, to go to a distant land, where all would be new and strange, and perhaps, too, hard for her. Yet at length all the farewells had been said, the last goodbye was spoken, and the two got into their sledge and the next instant the swift black steed flew off like an arrow, rushing on toward the land of Kalevala, leaving far behind them the gloomy Northland, which was yet so dear to the Rainbow-maiden, and which she was never to see again.

Three days they journeyed onward over hill and valley without stopping, and the third evening brought them in sight of Ilmarinen's smithy, and they could see the smoke rising from the chimneys of their home. There they found that they had been expected for a long time, and there was great rejoicing when their sledge drove up, with the birds singing merrily on its front, and all bright and happy.

Lakko, Ilmarinen's mother, received them at the door and welcomed the fair Rainbow-maiden most heartily, and p. 122 when the bridal pair had taken off their furs, she served them with the very best of food and drink—choicest bits of reindeer, wheaten biscuit, honey-cakes, and fish of all sorts, and the best of beer. And while they ate, the others, who had been old Louhi's guests, began to arrive, and soon there was a great feast going on, almost as great a one as there had been before at Louhi's.

While they were all feasting, Wainamoinen arose and began to sing again. This time he sang the praises of the bridegroom's father and mother, and the bride and groom, and ended up with praising the guests that were assembled there. Then he and many of the guests took their leave and journeyed off together to their homes. Three days they drove on together, and Wainamoinen kept on singing all the time, until suddenly his song was cut short, for his sledge ran into a birch-tree and was broken into pieces. But Wainamoinen considered the case and then said: 'Is there any one here who will go to Tuonela, to the Deathland, for the auger of Tuoni, that I may mend my sledge with it?' But no one would venture on so perilous a journey, so at length Wainamoinen went himself and obtained Tuoni's magic auger, and with its aid, on his return, he put together his magic sledge again.

Then he harnessed up his steed once more and galloped off to his home. Thus p. 123 ended Ilmarinen's wedding and the feasts that followed it.

These two stories took Antero's fancy, and he begged that 'Pappa Mikko would tell about some more times when they had good things to eat.'

But Father Mikko said: 'People can't be eating all the time, Antero, and I think the others would rather hear about what Lemminkainen did, when he heard of the feast and was not invited himself.'

Mimi cried 'Yes, yes!' and so the old man began.

THE ORIGIN OF THE SERPENT

 AS Lemminkainen was ploughing his fields one day, he heard the noise of sledges as if a vast number of people were on their way past. At once he guessed the reason, for they were the guests going to Ilmarinen's wedding, while he alone had not been invited. Then his face turned pale with anger, and he left his ploughing and hastened off to his house. When he arrived there, he asked his mother to give him a hearty meal, and after that he went to the bath-house and after the bath put on his finest garments, as if going to a feast.

His mother asked him where he was going and he told her that he was bound for the great feast that Louhi had prepared. But his mother tried to keep him from going, telling him that they did not want him there, or else they would have invited p. 125 him, but he answered: 'This sword with its sharp edges constantly reminds me that I am needed in distant Pohjola.' His mother spoke again, saying: 'Do not go, my dear son, for Death will meet thee thrice upon the way.' Lemminkainen replied that he did not fear Death, but would overcome him, but at the same time asked his mother what the first danger would be.

'When thou hast travelled for one day,' she replied, 'thou wilt come to a stream of fire, with a fiery cataract, and in the fire-fall a rock, and on the rock a fiery hill, and on its top an eagle made of flames, who devours all that approach him.'

Lemminkainen answered that he would easily pass this danger, and asked to know the second. His mother told him: 'When thou hast travelled two days, thou wilt come to a fiery pit filled with red-hot stones, and no one has ever been able to pass over it.'

But Lemminkainen thought but little of this second danger, and asked his mother to tell him what the third one was. She replied: 'When thou hast gone one day farther, and hast come to Pohjola, the wolf and the black bear will attack thee, and many hundred men have perished in their jaws.' But he told her how easily he would overcome them and then have conquered all the dangers of the journey. Then his mother added: 'There are three things still p. 126 to conquer. When thou reachest Louhi's dwelling, thou wilt find walls built of iron rising up to the sky, and surrounded by railings of spears on which are serpents and all manner of venomous creatures twisting and creeping about; and right before the gateway lies the largest of them all, longer than the rafters of a house. And beyond all this, thou wilt find great hosts of armed warriors, who have grown angry over their beer and they will certainly kill you. And if thou shouldst come into the courtyard, thou wilt find it full of sharp stakes, to hold the heads of those that go thither unbidden. Do not forget how thou once fared in Pohjola, that had I not saved thee thou wouldst now be at the bottom of Tuoni's river.'

Yet after she had warned him of all this, Lemminkainen would not be persuaded to remain at home, but put on his magic armour of copper and took his father's sword, and his own strongest bow. Then he had his steed hitched to a sledge and went out into the courtyard to drive off. There his mother bade him farewell and gave him some last words of advice, telling him that if he should come to the feast, to drink but half of his goblet of beer, for there were serpents in the other half, and to behave modestly and not to try to take the best of everything for himself. p. 127

When she had ended, Lemminkainen jumped upon his sledge, cracked his whip, and drove off like the wind. He had not gone far before a flock of wild birds flew across his road and dropped a few feathers on the ground. Lemminkainen stopped and picking them up put them carefully in his leather pouch, 'for,' he thought, 'no one knows what may happen.' As soon as he had picked up the feathers he was off again, but he had not gone far when his steed stopped in terror, for there, right in front of them, was a broad river of fire, and a fire-fall with a rock in the middle, and on the rock a fiery hill, and on the hill a flaming eagle.

The Eagle asked him whither he was going, and Lemminkainen replied that he was hurrying to Louhi's feast and begged the Eagle to let him pass. 'Truly thou shalt pass,' the Eagle answered, 'but only through the flames and down my throat.' But Lemminkainen was not dismayed. He took out the feathers from his pouch and rubbed them between his fingers, and presently there arose a whole flock of birds and flew straight down the eagle's mouth so that its hunger was satisfied, then Lemminkainen was able to pass over the river by the help of his magic, and to drive on his way.

He drove for another day and then his p. 128 horse suddenly stopped again in terror, for there was a huge pit full of fire right in front, which stretched as far as one could see to east and west. Yet Lemminkainen was not discouraged, but prayed to great Ukko, that he would send a great storm from all the four points of the compass, and fill the pit with snow. And the snow came and as it fell into the seething pit of fire it melted and formed a lake; and Lemminkainen quickly cast a spell upon this lake so that a solid bridge of ice was formed over it, and he drove over in perfect safety.

Thus the second danger was passed and he drove on more swiftly than ever. After another day's journey, when he had come near to Louhi's abode, his horse stopped again, trembling with fear. This time there were a fierce wolf and a great black bear in the road. But Lemminkainen put his hand into his leathern pouch and pulled out a tuft of wool. This he rubbed between his hands and breathed on it, and it changed into a whole flock of sheep, on which the bear and the wolf jumped and left Lemminkainen to pursue his journey in peace.

In a very short time he had reached Louhi's house. But there he found the great wall of iron and the fence of spears and the horrible snakes and lizards that his mother had told him of. Yet he pulled out his magic broad sword and cut an opening p. 129 through the wall and the fence of spears and the mass of serpents, and passed through to the gateway. There he found a huge serpent with a hundred eyes, each as large as bowls, and a thousand tongues long as javelins, and teeth like hatchets. Lemminkainen sang one spell, but it was not powerful enough, and the huge monster started to rush at him and seize him in its awful mouth. But Lemminkainen just in time began to sing a stronger spell.

For evil things cannot bear to have their wicked origin told, and if therefore one sings the source of any evil, one makes it harmless at once, so Lemminkainen sang: 'If thou wilt not give room for me to pass, I will sing of thy evil origin, will tell how thy horrid head was made. Suoyatar, thy evil mother, once spat upon the waves of the sea. The spittle was rocked by the waves and warmed by the sun, until after a long time it was washed ashore. There the daughters of Ukko, the Creator, saw it, and said: "What would happen if great Ukko were to breathe the breath of life into this writhing, senseless mass?" But Ukko overheard them and said: "Naught but evil comes from evil, therefore I will not give it life."

'Now, wicked Lempo heard what Ukko had said, and he himself breathed into it the breath of life, and shaped it to the form p. 130 of a serpent, adding to the spittle all manner of evil things, every poisonous plant and thing from the Deathland. This was thine origin, O Serpent, vilest thing of all creation; therefore clear the pathway that I may enter the halls of the hostess Louhi.'

Thus sang Lemminkainen, and the serpent uncoiled itself and crawled away, while Ahti himself went on through the gateway.

THE UNWELCOME GUEST

THUS Lemminkainen came unbidden to Louhi's abode, but he had arrived too late for the feast. He entered the house with such a mighty tread that the floors bent under him and the walls and ceilings creaked as he advanced. Louhi's husband was seated in the guest-room, and Lemminkainen said to him: 'The same greeting to thee that thou givest to me! Are there food and beer here for a stranger and barley for a hungry steed?'

Louhi's husband answered: 'I have never yet refused a place in my stables for a stranger's horse, and if thou wilt act honestly there is a place for thee between the iron kettles.'

Lemminkainen said: 'When my father Lempo comes to a house as a guest, he is well received and given the place of honour. p. 132 Why should I, his son, be put between the pots and kettles to be covered with soot?' With these words he walked up to the table, and taking his seat he waited to be served.

Then Louhi said to him: 'O Lemminkainen, thou wert not invited hither, and I feel that thou bringest sorrow with thee. All our dinner was eaten and our beer drunk yesterday, and we have nothing left for thee.'

This made Lemminkainen very angry, and he replied: 'O toothless mistress of Pohjola, thou hast managed thy feast very badly, for thou hast had delicacies of every sort for the others, who gave but trifling presents, while for me, who have sent the most of all, thou hast nothing at all after my long journey.'

Then Louhi called up one of her meanest servants and bade her serve the guest. And there came a little short woman, who made ready a soup out of fish-bones and fish-heads and crusts of bread and turnip-stalks, and brought him the worst of the servants' beer to quench his thirst with. Lemminkainen looked into the pitchers of beer, and saw snakes and worms and lizards floating about in them. This made him furiously angry, yet he resolved to drink the beer at any rate, and then to punish them for their evil treatment of him. p. 133 So he drew a fish-hook out of his magic wallet, and with it he caught all the evil creatures in the beer and killed them with his sword, and drank the beer.

When he had done this, he turned to the host and upbraided him for his bad treatment, and finally said that as the Pohjola folk could not treat guests decently, perhaps he could purchase good beer at least. At this Louhi's husband grew angry and conjured up a little lake in the floor at Lemminkainen's feet, and bade him quench his thirst at that. But Lemminkainen conjured up a bull with gold and silver horns, that drank up all the water. Then Louhi's husband conjured up a wolf to devour the bull, but Ahti called up a rabbit to draw off the wolf's attention. Next the host conjured up a dog to eat the rabbit, but Ahti drew away the dog by means of a squirrel that he called up by his magic. At that the host made a golden marten to catch the squirrel, and Lemminkainen a scarlet-coloured fox which ate the golden marten. Next the host conjured a hen to distract the scarlet fox, and Lemminkainen made a hawk to tear the hen to pieces.

Then old Louhi's husband cried: 'We shall never be happy here until thou art driven out, O evil Ahti,' and with these words he drew his sword and challenged Lemminkainen to combat. So Ahti drew p. 134 his sword also, and when the two were measured, they found that Ahti's was the shorter by half an inch.

Then Lemminkainen said to his host: 'Although thou hast the longer sword, yet thou shalt begin the fight.'

After this they placed themselves in position, and the host of Pohjola began. But so powerful was Lemminkainen's magic that he only hit the walls and floor and rafters, but could not touch Ahti himself. Then Lemminkainen said sneeringly: 'What harm have the walls and rafters done, that thou shouldst cut them to pieces. But come, let us go out into the courtyard, that the hall may not be covered with blood.'

So they went out into the yard, and there they spread out an ox-hide, and took up their places on it to continue the fight. Lemminkainen again allowed the host to begin, and the latter struck three mighty blows, but still could not harm Ahti. Then the battle began in real earnest, and the sparks flew from their swords until it seemed as if there were a sheet of flame flowing from Lemminkainen's sword and down upon the head and shoulders of his opponent. And when he saw this, Lemminkainen said: 'O thou son of Pohjola, see how thy neck is shining like the ocean at dawn.'

The other turned without thinking, to see what it was, and quick as lightning Lemmin p. 135 kainen whirled his sword round his head, and with one blow cut off the host's head as easily as one cuts the top from a turnip, and the head rolled along on the ground. In the yard were hundreds of sharp stakes, and on all but one there was a human head. So Lemminkainen quickly took the host's head and stuck it on the empty stake, and then went into the house and ordered Louhi to bring him water to wash his hands, as he had just slain her husband.

But Louhi hastened out and called in hundreds of armed warriors to avenge her husband's death. And in a very short time Lemminkainen saw that he must either flee or else be killed if he remained.

THE ISLE OF REFUGE

LEMMINKAINEN hastened from Louhi's house and looked around for his sledge and steed to escape from the Pohjola men. But both had disappeared, and in their place he found only a clump of willows. As he stood there, wondering what he should do next, the noise of armed men running together grew louder and louder, and he knew that they would soon reach him. So Lemminkainen changed himself into an eagle, and rose up into the clouds. As he flew towards the south he met a gray hawk flying northward, and called to it: 'O Gray Hawk, fly to Pohjola and tell the warriors of the Northland that they will never catch the Eagle, Lemminkainen, ere he reaches his home in distant Kalevala.'

Then he flew on home and taking on p. 137 again his own form, he went to his mother's house. When she saw the troubled look in his face, she guessed that some great danger threatened him, and began to ask him if it were this, or that, or the other that troubled him, but to all her questions he answered 'no.' At length she bade him tell her, then, what his trouble was, and he replied: 'All the men of Northland are sharpening their swords and spears to kill thy unlucky son Ahti, for I have slain the host of Pohjola, Louhi's husband, in a quarrel, and the men of Northland will soon come hither to avenge it.'

His mother then reminded him how she had warned him of the journey and its troubles, and asked him where he was going to take refuge. Lemminkainen replied that he did not know, and asked his mother to help him, and she answered: 'If I should turn thee into a tree, thou might be cut down for firewood. Or if into a berry, the maidens might pluck thee. Or if to a fish, thou would never have a happy life. But if thou wilt swear to me not to go to war again for sixty years, then I will tell thee of a distant isle, far off across the ocean, where thou mayst rest in safety.'

So Lemminkainen gave his promise, on his honour, not to fight for sixty years, and then his mother told him how to find the isle of refuge. He must sail across nine p. 138 seas and in the middle of the tenth he would come to the island, where his father had once taken refuge long before. There he must stay until the third year was come, and then he might return to his home.

Lemminkainen took enough provisions in his boat for a long journey, and then bidding farewell to his mother and his home he sailed away. When he had raised the linen sails, he called up a fair wind to drive him onward, and for three months he sailed on without a moment's rest, until at length he reached the magic Isle of Refuge.

First, he asked the people of the island if there was room there for his boat, and on receiving their consent he drew it up out of the water. Next he asked them if he might take refuge and conceal himself there, and they granted this too; but when he asked for a little ground to cultivate, and a place in the forest to cut down the trees, they told him that the whole island had long ago been divided up amongst them, and that he must live in one of their houses if he wished to stay on the island.

But Lemminkainen was not satisfied with this, and told them that he only wished to be allowed to go into the forest and sing some few magic songs there, and this they willingly allowed him to do. So he went into the forest and began to sing the most wondrous spells, making oak-trees to grow p. 139 up around him, and on each branch an acorn, and on each acorn sat a cuckoo. Then the cuckoos began to sing, and gold fell from every beak, and silver from their wings, and copper from their feathers, until the isle was abundantly supplied with precious metals. Then Lemminkainen sang again, and turned the sand to gems and the pebbles into pearls, and he covered the whole island with flowers, and made little lakes with gold and silver ducks swimming in them, until every one was delighted, and the maidens most of all.

Then Ahti said: 'If I were in a fine castle I would conjure up the most wonderful feasts and sing the grandest songs you have ever heard.' No sooner had he said this than they led him to their finest castle, and there he conjured up a splendid feast, with knives and forks and all the dishes made of gold and silver. From this time on Ahti was treated as an honoured guest, and spent his time most delightfully. In every village on the island were seven castles, and in each castle were seven daughters, and all of these made Lemminkainen welcome as he went from one to another according to his fancy. Thus he spent the whole of his years of exile; but there was one maid, old and ugly, and living in a remote village, whom he neglected.

At length the time of his return was come, and he made up his mind to leave. But p. 140 just as he had decided to go, the maid whom he had neglected came to him and bade him beware, for she was going to take revenge for his slighting her; but Lemminkainen scarcely heard her, for he was so busy thinking about his journey home. But the maiden went around to all the men of the island, and told them evil stories about Lemminkainen, and then she went and burned his boat.

The next morning Lemminkainen started off to bid his friends the maidens farewell, but he had not gone far before he saw the men getting their weapons ready to come and attack him, and he saw that he must fly immediately if he wished to escape alive. So he hastened down to his boat, but when he reached it there were only the ashes left. At first he did not know what to do, but he spied seven broken pieces of planks and a few fragments from a broken distaff, and taking these he began to sing some mystic spells over them. No sooner had he finished his incantations than a magic boat stood ready before him, and he got into it and sailed away. But before he was far from the shore all the maidens came down to the beach and began to weep and beg him to come back and dwell with them for ever. But Lemminkainen answered them that he felt a great longing to see his home once more and his mother, yet that he was truly p. 141 sorrowful to leave them, but it must be so. And so he sailed on until the isle was out of sight.

The boat sailed on and on for two days and nights, but on the third day came a mighty storm-wind, and tossed the vessel about until it broke all in pieces, and left Lemminkainen struggling in the waters. He swam for long days and nights, struggling with the waves, until at length he reached a rocky point projecting out into the ocean. There he landed and soon found his way to a castle that was built upon the rocks. He told the mistress of the castle how he had been in the water for days and days, and was almost perishing from hunger, and she, being a kind-hearted woman, gave him a splendid feast of bread and butter, veal and bacon, and fish and honey-cakes, and when he had eaten that and rested, she gave him a new boat, loaded with provisions, in which to finish his journey.

So off he sailed again, and after many weary days of sailing he at length reached his beloved island-home. But when he landed and went up to where the house had stood, there was not a sign of anything left. The whole place was all overgrown with trees and bushes.

Then Lemminkainen sat down and began to weep; but it was not for the loss of his home and all his riches that he wept but p. 142 for his beloved mother. As he sat there he caught sight of an eagle flying in the air above, and Ahti asked him if he knew what had happened to his mother. But the eagle could only tell him that his people had all perished long go. Next he asked the raven, and the raven told him that his people had been killed by his enemies from Pohjola.

On hearing this Lemminkainen began again to mourn her loss, and to look about for some dear relic that he might keep in remembrance of her. But as he looked he suddenly came on a faint pathway leading away from the house, and on it he saw the prints of light feet. He began to follow it eagerly, over hill and valley until he reached the gloomy forest. There it led him to a hidden glade, right in the middle of the island, and there he found a humble cabin, and his gray-haired mother weeping in it.

Ahti cried aloud for joy at the sight of her, and then he told her how he had mourned her as dead. She asked him in return how he had spent those years on the Isle of Refuge, and he told her all; how charming the life there was, and how he had enjoyed himself there, but that at the end all the men of the isle had come to hate him, because the maidens admired him so much, and how through their jealousy and p. 143 the hatred of the one maid whom he had neglected, he had nearly lost his life. And when he had ended his story they both gave thanks to great Ukko that they had found each other again.

THE FROST-FIEND

WHEN the next day began to dawn, Lemminkainen went to the beach, that was hidden behind a projecting point, where his vessels lay. He found them still there, but as he approached he heard the rigging wailing in the wind, and saying: 'Must we lie here for ever and rot, since Ahti has sworn not to go to war for sixty long years?'

Then Lemminkainen cried out to his vessels: 'Mourn no more, my good warships, for soon ye shall be filled with warriors and hastening to the battle.' When he had uttered these words he hurried back to his mother and bade her sorrow no longer over the insult that the Pohjola warriors had offered to her, for he was going now to make war on them in order to punish them for it.

His mother, when she heard his intention, p. 145 besought him earnestly not to go to war and break his oath to her, for some great misfortune would surely come upon him. But he paid no heed to her, and went to seek his friend Kura to accompany him on his expedition. When he came to the isle on which Kura lived, he went up to the house and said: 'O my dear friend Kura, dost thou not remember the time when we fought together long ago against the men of dismal Northland? Come with me now and be my companion in another war against them.'

Now Kura's father was sitting by the window, whittling out a javelin, and his mother was near the door skimming milk, and his brother and sisters were also working near by. And all of them cried out that Kura could not go to war, for he was but lately married, and they bade Lemminkainen leave him.

But Kura himself jumped up from where he was lying before the fire, and began to put on his armour in great haste. On his helmet were wolves of bronze, and a horse on each javelin. Then Kura took his mighty spear, and going forth into the court he hurled it towards the north; and it flew on and on, whistling through the air, until at length it fell upon the earth of the distant Northland. And after this Kura touched his javelin against Lemminkainen's spear and promised to be his faithful comrade in p. 146 the expedition. So the two great warriors made all needful preparation and set forth to sail to dismal Pohjola.

But Louhi knew by magic art that they were coming, and she called the Black-frost to her, and gave him these commands: 'Hasten forth, O Black-frost, and freeze all the wide sea. Freeze Lemminkainen's vessel fast in the ice, and freeze the magician himself in his vessel, so that he may never more awaken from his icy sleep until I myself may choose to free him.'

So the Black-frost hastened off to do her bidding. And first he stripped the leaves off the trees and took all the colour from the flowers on his way to the seashore. When he reached the shore, the first night he froze all the rivers that empty into the sea and the waters along the shore, but he did not touch the open sea that night. But on the second night he froze all the sea, and the ice kept growing thicker and thicker all around Lemminkainen's vessel, until at last the Black-frost even began to freeze Lemminkainen's hands and feet and ears.

But when Lemminkainen felt this he began to sing an incantation against the Black-frost, saying: 'Black-frost, evil child of the Northland and only son of Winter, thou mayst freeze the trees and waters and the very stones, — but let me be in peace. Freeze the iron mountains till they burst in sunder; p. 147 freeze Wuoksi and Imatra, but do not try to harm me, for I will sing thine origin and make thee powerless. For thou wert born on the borders of the ever-dismal Northland, and wert fed by crawling snakes. The Northwind rocked thee to sleep in the marshes, and thus thou grew, a thing of evil, and at last the name of Frost was given thee. And as thou became larger, thou didst learn to rend the trees in winter and to cover all the lakes with ice. But if thou wilt not leave me now, I will cast thee into Lempo's fiery hearth, and will lay thee on the anvil, that Ilmarinen may pound thee to pieces with his mighty hammer.'

Now the Frost-fiend knew how great a magician Lemminkainen was, and therefore he agreed that he would leave the two warriors unharmed, but keep their ship frozen up as it was. And so Ahti and Kura had to leave their vessel and journey over the ice to land. At length they reached the country called Starvation-land, and there they found a house, but there was no food in it. So they went on still farther, over hill and valley, and as they went, Lemminkainen gathered soft moss from the tree-trunks and made stockings of it to keep their feet warm.

On and on they went, seeking for some pathway to guide them, but all was one snow-covered wilderness. Then Kura said: p. 148 'Alas, O Ahti; we came hither to take vengeance on the men of Pohjola, but I fear that we shall leave our own bones here, and our flesh be food for eagles and ravens. We shall never learn the pathway that can guide us to our homes. My poor mother will never know what has become of me—whether I have perished in the heat of battle, or on some lonely hill, or in some dismal forest. She can only mourn me as one dead, and sit and weep bitter tears.'

Then Lemminkainen said: 'My aged mother, think of our former happy days, when all went well and all was joy and happiness. But now sorrow and misfortune are come upon me, yet shall we not despair; for we are young and strong, and will give way neither to hunger nor to evil sorcerers, but will use the prayer my father used to pray, saying: "Guard us, O thou great Creator; shield us in thine arms, and give us of thy wisdom. Be our guardian and our Father, that thy children may not wander from the path which thou hast given them."'

Then when Lemminkainen had finished speaking, he took his cares and made fleet coursers of them, and the reins he made of days of evil, and from his pains he made the saddles. Then he and Kura galloped off each to his own home, and thus Lemminkainen was once more returned to his aged mother's arms. Now let us leave him p. 149 there, and Kura with his bride and kinsfolk, and speak hereafter of other heroes.

Thus Father Mikko ended, adding: 'And I think we must stop now for the night, for it is getting late.' Then they had supper, and it was not long before all of them had gone to bed and were sound asleep.

Early the next morning they were all awakened by a dull thud and a smothered shout. Erik and Father Mikko jumped up and lit a lantern, and then hurried to the door, which stood open. They had dug a passage-way out through the snow the day before, and they saw that the walls of snow had just caved in, and sticking out of the middle of the heap was a pair of small legs waving about wildly in the air.

The next minute they had pulled out the owner of the legs, and little Antero stood before them, looking very much frightened and very foolish too. He had his snow-shoes and some meat with him, and managed to explain, between his sobs, that he had intended to go and hunt for reindeer in Lapland, the way Lemminkainen did in the story, but his snow-shoe had caught in the wall and disaster had overtaken him. The would-be hero was promptly taken in charge by Mother Stina, and soon all was quiet again. p. 150

When they went out the next morning, they found that the snow had long since stopped, but the wind was blowing so hard and it was so bitterly cold, that Father Mikko was easily persuaded to stay another day.

After dinner they settled down exactly as the day before, Mimi in 'Pappa' Mikko's lap again, and in a few minutes he began to tell them some more of his wonderful stories.

'I will tell you about some one you have not heard of yet,' Father Mikko said; 'about *Kullervo*, though I am sure you will none of you like Kullervo himself — but yet the story itself may be interesting.' So he began.

144

MIMI IN HOLIDAY DRESS.

KULLERVO'S BIRTH

MANY ages ago there was a mother who had three sons, and one of them grew up to be a prosperous merchant, but the other two were carried off — one to distant Pohjola and one to Karjala. And the one in Pohjola was named Untamo, but the one in Karjala was called Kalerwoinen.

One day Untamo set his nets near Kalerwoinen's home to catch salmon, but in the evening Kalerwoinen came by and took all the fish out of the nets and carried them off home. When Untamo found it out he went to his brother, and soon they fell to blows; but neither could conquer the other, though they gave one another sound beatings. After this had happened, Kalerwoinen sowed some barley near Untamo's barns; and Untamo's sheep broke into the field and ate the barley, and then Kalerwoinen's p. 152 dog killed the sheep. This made Untamo so angry that he collected a great army and marched against his brother to put him and all his tribe to death. And when they reached Kalerwoinen's home they burned all the houses and killed every one except Kalerwoinen's daughter Untamala.

Now not long after this a child was born to Untamala, and she named him Kullervo. Then they laid the fatherless infant in the cradle and began to rock him, but he began at once to make the cradle rock without assistance, and he rocked for three whole days, so hard that his hair stood quite on end. On the third day he began to kick until he had burst his swaddling clothes, and then he crept out of the cradle and broke that also in pieces. When Kullervo was only three months old he began to speak, and the first words which he uttered were these: 'When I have grown big and strong I will avenge the murder of my grandfather Kalerwoinen and his people.'

At this Untamo was greatly alarmed, and took counsel with his people as to what should be done with the child. At length they hit upon a plan. They took the child and bound him firmly in a willow basket and then put him in the lake among the bulrushes. After three days had passed they went to see if he were dead, but he had broken loose from the basket and was sitting p. 153 on the waves, fishing with a copper rod and a golden line; so they took him back again to the house. Next Untamo ordered a great heap of dried brushwood to be collected together, and a pile was made higher than the tree-tops; on the top of this they set the boy and then set fire to the pile. It burned three whole days, and then Untamo sent men to see if the child was dead; but they found him sitting in the middle of the fire raking the coals together with a copper rod, and not a hair of his head was even singed.

Then they took him home and considered again how they should kill him, and this time they took him and crucified him on an oak-tree. And on the third day they came and found that he had painted an armed warrior on every leaf, made fast though he was to the tree, and so they took him down and brought him home again. This time they saw that they could not harm him, so Untamo told him that he would take him as a servant, and that if he did well he should be paid well.

When Kullervo had grown a little, he was set to take care of a baby, and was given very careful instructions as to how to rock it and attend to all its wants; but the cruel Kullervo treated it harshly, and in the evening killed it and burned the cradle in the fire. So Untamo was afraid to give p. 154 him any further employment about the house, but bade him go out and cut down the forest on the mountain side. Then Kullervo went to the smith and bade him make a huge axe of copper, and when it was ready he spent one day in sharpening it and another in making the handle, and then hastened off to the forest. There he chose the biggest tree on all the mountain side and felled it at one blow. Six more huge trees were cut down just as easily, but then Kullervo grew disgusted with the work, and pronounced a curse over the whole mountain, and stopped working.

So when Untamo came in the evening to see how he was getting on, and found only seven trees felled, he saw that he must set Kullervo to some other task. The next day, therefore, he took him into a field and bade him build a fence round it. As soon as Untamo was gone, Kullervo set to work, using whole trees and raising the fence higher than the clouds; and when he had finished there was no gate to enter by, and the fence was so high that no one could climb over it. When Untamo came and saw what he had done, and that no one could now get into the field, he told Kullervo that he was unfitted for such work, and must go and thresh the rye and barley.

Then Kullervo made a flail and set to work. And he threshed so hard that all p. 155 the grain was beaten to powder and the straw was broken up into useless pieces. But when Untamo saw this, he grew very angry, and cried out that Kullervo was a wretched workman who spoiled whatever he touched, and the next day he took him off and sold him to the blacksmith Ilmarinen in distant Karjala. And the price Ilmarinen paid was three old worn-out kettles, seven worthless sickles, and three old scythes and hoes and axes, surely quite enough for such a fellow as Kullervo.

KULLERVO AND ILMARINEN'S WIFE

AS soon as the purchase was completed, Kullervo asked Ilmarinen and his wife to give him some work for the next day. So
they decided to make him a shepherd. But the wife, once the Rainbow-maiden, did not like the new servant, so she baked him a
cheat-loaf—a very thick loaf, half of barley, half of oatmeal, and
with a great flint-stone in the centre, and around the flint-stone was
melted butter. Then she gave it to Kullervo and told him not to eat it
until he was out on the pasture-ground.

The next morning Ilmarinen's wife showed Kullervo the cattle,
and bade him take them to the open glades among the forests,
where they would find food in abundance. Then she addressed a
prayer to Ukko that he would guard the flock in case the shepherd
p. 157 should neglect them. And she sought the aid too of all the
goddesses of the forest and the daughters of summer and the spirits
of the fountains and the brooks, to care for her cattle and watch over
them. And she also sang a spell to keep away the bear from coming
and devouring them. And when all these prayers and spells were
ended she sent Kullervo off with the herds.

Kullervo drove them off to their pastures in the woods, carrying
his lunch in a basket on his arm. And as he walked he sang of his
hard lot as a slave, and how he was given only the scraps and crusts
to eat, while his master and mistress fed on honey-cakes and wheat-
en biscuit. At length the time came for him to eat his luncheon, and
he sat down and drew the cheat-loaf from the basket. But instead of
eating it at once he turned it carefully over and over in his hands,
and thought: 'Many loaves are fine to look at on the outside, but are
nothing but chaff inside,' and he drew out his knife to try the loaf.

This knife was the one thing that his mother had kept of all her
father's possessions, and Kullervo looked upon it as something
sacred. Now as he plunged it into the cheat-loaf it hit right upon the

151

hard flint in the centre and broke in several pieces. Then Kullervo sat down and began to weep over his loss, and to ponder how he should p. 158 revenge it. But a raven was sitting in a tree near by and overhead him talking to himself, and the raven said: 'Why art thou so distressed, Kullervo? Drive the herd away, one half to the wolves' and the other half to the bears' dens, so that they may all be devoured. And then when it is time to return home call together the wolves and bears and make them look like cattle, by thy magic art, and drive them home for thy mistress to milk. Thus thou wilt repay this insult.'

At these words Kullervo jumped up and did as the raven had said. And when the sun was setting in the west, Kullervo hastened homeward, driving bears and wolves before him, but by a magic spell he made them look like cattle. And as he went, he said to them: 'Seize my hateful mistress when she comes to milk the cattle, and tear and rend her in pieces.' And he took a cow-horn and made a bugle of it and blew till the hills rang, to announce his return.

When he reached the cow-yard, Ilmarinen's wife greeted him joyfully, for it was late and she had feared that something had happened. And she told her oldest maid-servant to go and milk the cows as she herself was busy. But Kullervo said: 'Thou shouldst go thyself, for the cows are in better condition to-night than they have p. 159 ever been before.' And so she went, and when she saw them she cried out in wonder: 'Truly my cattle are beautiful to-night, for their hair glistens like the fur of lynxes, and is soft as ermine skin.'

With these words she seated herself to begin milking, but all at once the wolves and bears appeared in their true shapes and began to tear her to pieces. Then she cried out to Kullervo, when she saw what he had done, but he answered: 'If I have done evil thou hast done still greater evil, for thou hast baked a stone inside my bread, and I have broken on it my knife, the only relic of my mother's people.'

Then Ilmarinen's wife began to beg him to aid her, and promised him the best of everything to eat, and that he should never have to work again. But Kullervo would not listen to her prayers, but rejoiced at her agony, and then the wolves and bears made one more onset, and she fell and died. Such was the end of the beauteous

Rainbow-maiden, for whom so many had wooed, and who had become the pride and joy of Kalevala.

KULLERVO'S LIFE AND DEATH

 THEN Kullervo hastened off, before Ilmarinen should come home and find out what had happened. And after he was at a safe distance he began to play upon the bugle he had made, until Ilmarinen ran out of his smithy to see who it could be, and there before him in the courtyard Ilmarinen saw the body of his wife and learned what had happened: and he sat down and wept bitterly, for all the joy of his life was now gone from him.

But Kullervo hastened on, and as he went he mourned his hard lot. When he had gone a little way he met an old witch on the road, and she asked him whither he was going. 'I shall journey to the dismal Northland,' answered Kullervo, 'there to slay the wicked Untamo, who has killed all my kinsfolk.' Then the witch said: 'Thou art wrong, for thy father and thy sisters escaped p. 161 from Untamo's wrath, and now thy mother has joined them and they are living happily together on the distant borders of Kalevala.' And when Kullervo begged her to tell him the way to them she did so, and he hastened off to find them.

At length he reached his parents' abode, but at first they did not recognise him. But when he spoke to his mother she knew him at once, and embraced him and kissed him, and made him welcome in his new home. And then they related to one another all that had happened in the years they had been apart, and his mother ended by saying: 'Praised be Ukko that thou hast come back to us; but there is yet one absent one—thy eldest sister strayed away many years ago, hunting berries on the hills, and we have never seen or heard of her since.'

So Kullervo settled down to live with his parents, and began to work with the others. The first day they all went out to fish for salmon, and Kullervo was put at the oars to row their boat. Then he asked whether he should row with all his strength, or only a little part of it, and they told him that he could not pull too hard. So he put forth all his giant's strength, and in a minute the boat was all broken to pieces.

His father said: 'I see that thou art too clumsy to row; perhaps thou wilt do better to drive the salmon into the nets.' And p. 162 Kullervo asked again whether he should use all his strength, and he received the same answer as before. So he set to work beating the water to scare the fish into the net; but he beat so hard that he mixed all the mud on the bottom with the water, and pounded the salmon all to pulp and destroyed all the nets.

Then his father saw that he was not fit for such work, so he sent him off to pay the yearly taxes. Kullervo did so, and after he had paid them he started off in his sledge to drive home again. He had not driven far when he met a lovely maiden, whom he asked to get into his sledge and come with him to his home and marry him. But she made fun of him, and he drove off in anger. When he had driven still farther he met another maiden, still more lovely than the first, and this one he at length persuaded to get into his sledge and come home with him and marry him. But when they had driven along for two days towards his home, the maiden asked him about his kinsfolk, and he told her that he was Kalervo's son.

No sooner had the maiden heard this than she gave a great cry of anguish and cried out: 'Alas, then, thou art my brother! For I am Kalervo's daughter, who wandered off one day to pick berries and never returned,' and with these words she jumped p. 163 from the sledge and hastened weeping to a river near by. There she plunged beneath the icy waters and was never seen again alive, but her lifeless body floated down to the black river of Tuoni.

But Kullervo unharnessed his steed from the sledge and galloped off home and there related to his mother all that had occurred, and how he had unknowingly been the cause of his sister's death, and when he had finished his story, he added: 'Woe is me that I did not die long ago. But now I must hasten off to gloomy Pohjola, there to slay the wicked Untamo, and myself be also slain.' Having said this he also made ready his armour and ground his broadsword until it was as sharp as a razor. But before he went, he asked his father and brother and sister and mother if they would grieve when they heard of his death. And all but his mother told him that they would never sorrow over the death of such an evil fellow. But his mother alone said that, in spite of all the evil he had done, her mother's love was still strong and that she would weep over him for years to come.

Thereupon Kullervo went forth on his journey to the icy North-land, but before he had gone far a messenger came and told him that his father was dead and asked Kullervo to come back and help bury him, p. 164 but he would not come. And a little later he was told of the death of his brother and then of his sister, and last of all of his mother. Still he refused to come to bury any of them, only, when the news of his mother's death reached him, he mourned that he had not been with her in her last moments, and bade the servants bury her with every possible honour and respect.

Now as he neared the home of Untamo's tribe, he prayed to Ukko to endow his sword with magic powers, so that Untamo and all his people might be surely slain. And Ukko did as he had asked, and with the magic sword Kullervo slew, single-handed, all Untamo's people, and burned all their villages to ashes, leaving behind him only dead bodies and smoking ruins.

Then he hastened home, and found that it was only too true that all his family had died while he was away; and he went out to his mother's grave and wept over it. But as he wept, his mother spoke to him from the grave and bade him let their old dog lead him into the forest to the home of the wood-nymphs, who would care for him. So Kullervo set off, led by the faithful dog. But on the way they came to the grassy mound where Kullervo had met his long-lost sister, and there he found that even the grass and the flowers and the trees were weeping. Suddenly overcome with sorrow, p. 165 he drew forth his magic sword from out its scabbard, and, bidding a last farewell to all the world, he thrust the handle firmly into the earth and threw himself upon the sword-point, so that it pierced his heart. Thus ended the evil life of Kullervo.

They were all silent for a moment when the sad story of Kullervo's life and death was ended, and then Mimi said: 'I wish you'd tell us about nice men like Ilmarinen and Wainamoinen, Pappa Mikko; Kullervo was real hateful.'

'Well, then, I will tell you of what Ilmarinen did when he had lost his wife, the Rainbow-maiden,' — and the old man began.

ILMARINEN'S BRIDE OF GOLD

 AFTER Ilmarinen's wife had been so cruelly slain, he wept for three whole days and nights without ceasing. And after that for three months he did not go into his smithy nor even so much as lift his hammer from the ground. And as he mourned he cried: 'Woe is me, for all is weariness and sorrow now that my dear wife is slain, and there is no more rest for me in my home.'

But after the three months of mourning were past, Ilmarinen went out and dug up a great quantity of gold and silver and cut down thirty sledge-loads of birch-trees, which he burnt to charcoal. Then he put the charcoal in the bottom of his furnace and laid a large piece of gold and a still larger piece of silver on top, and closing the furnace, he started the fire and set the workmen to blowing the bellows; but the p. 167 men were lazy and let the fire go out. So Ilmarinen drove them all away and began to blow the fire by magic spells alone. Three days he worked the bellows by his magic spells, and on the evening of the third day he looked inside the furnace, hoping to see an image rising from the melted gold and silver. And there came forth a lovely lamb all gold and silver, and every one admired its beauty save Ilmarinen, who said: 'Get back into the furnace, for I only desire a beauteous bride, born of the melted gold and silver.'

So he threw the lamb back into the furnace and added still more gold and silver and other magic metals, and then set his workmen to blow the bellows again. But they proved lazy this time too, and he had once more to use his magic spells to blow the fire. Again he looked into the furnace, on the evening of the third day, and this time there arose a colt of gold and silver and with hoofs of shining copper. Every one admired the beautiful colt save Ilmarinen, who threw it back into the furnace.

Once more he added gold and silver and set the workmen to blow the bellows, but they neglected their work this time too. Then he blew the fire by magic, and cast other magic spells over the furnace, so that the gold and silver should grow into a lovely maiden. When he looked into the furnace p. 168 on the evening of the third day, he saw at last the figure of a maiden rising from the flames, but it had neither feet nor hands nor ears. So Ilmarinen took her from the fire and forged unceasingly until feet and hands and ears were all completed, and the maiden was now the most beautiful that any one had ever seen, but yet she could not walk, nor talk, nor see, nor hear.

But Ilmarinen carried the golden maiden out of the smithy and took her to the bath-room where he washed the golden and silver image and then took it and laid it in his couch, in his wife's place. That night he heaped up bear-skins and rugs of all kinds on top of the bed, hoping that the image would come to life from the warmth, but it was all in vain, and Ilmarinen was almost frozen himself when he rose next morning. Then he said to himself: 'Surely this lovely maiden was not meant to be my bride. I will take her to Wainamoinen, and perhaps she may come to life for him.'

So off he went and offered the beautiful image to Wainamoinen, telling him that he had brought a lovely maiden to be Wainamoinen's bride now in his old age. But Wainamoinen, after praising the image's beauty, said: 'My dear brother Ilmarinen, it is better to throw this image back into thy furnace, and to forge from the melted metal a thousand useful trinkets. For I will p. 169 never wed an image made of gold and silver.'

And then Wainamoinen turned to those of his people who were standing near by, and said to them: 'Never bow to any image made of gold or silver, for they cannot see, nor hear, nor speak, and they will only bring you sorrow.'

ILMARINEN'S FRUITLESS WOOING

 SO Ilmarinen cast the maid of gold into a corner of his smithy and harnessed up his sledge and drove off to the dismal Northland, to ask Louhi to give him another of her daughters in marriage. Three days he journeyed, and on the evening of the third he reached old Louhi's home.

Louhi asked him how her daughter, the Rainbow-maiden, fared, and Ilmarinen, with hanging head and sorrowful face, told how his poor wife had perished, and ended up his story by asking Louhi to give him her next fairest daughter to be his wife. But Louhi grew angry and upbraided him with not having guarded her other daughter, and thus being guilty of her death, and she scornfully refused to give him another of her daughters.

But Ilmarinen went into the house in p. 171 great anger and there addressed Louhi's next fairest daughter, begging her to come to his home with him and become his wife. The maid replied: 'I will never marry the man who has been the cause of my dear sister's death. And even if I were to marry I would wish a nobler suitor than a mere blacksmith.' Then Ilmarinen grew pale with anger, and seizing the maiden in his mighty arms he rushed off to his sledge and drove off like the wind before any one could stop him.

The poor maid wept and begged Ilmarinen to release her and to let her die by the roadside, rather than to take her thus to his home. 'If thou wilt not release me,' she said, 'I will change into a salmon and escape thee.' But Ilmarinen told her that he would pursue her in the shape of a pike. Then the maiden said, first, that she would become an ermine, but Ilmarinen told her he would turn into a snake and catch her; and then she said that she would become a swallow, but Ilmarinen threatened to become an eagle.

So they drove on and on, and the maiden wept the whole time, and begged Ilmarinen to let her go, even if it were only to die in the snow, but he refused and grew more and more angry at her obstinacy. At length they reached Ilmarinen's home and he took the maiden into the house. But p. 172 here, seeing there was no hope of escape, she determined to make him so angry that he would kill her and thus she would be freed from him. So she began to make fun of him and to scorn him and laugh at him, until at length Ilmarinen was in such a rage that he scarcely knew what he was doing, and drew his sword to kill her.

But the sword refused to do this cruel deed, saying: 'I was born to drink the blood of warriors, but not of such a pure and lovely maid as this.' So Ilmarinen, being unable to kill her, began to weave a magic spell about her, and in a few minutes she changed all of a sudden into a seagull, and flew off screaming towards the sea-cliffs.

And when he had done this, Ilmarinen went out and got into his sledge and drove off to his brother Wainamoinen. When he arrived, Wainamoinen asked him why he was so sad, and whether all was well in Pohjola. To this Ilmarinen replied: 'Why should not all be well in Pohjola? They have the Sampo there, and until it leaves them they will always prosper.' And then Wainamoinen asked him of the maiden whom he had gone to woo. 'I have turned that hateful maid into a seagull,' Ilmarinen answered, frowning, 'and now she flies shrieking above the rolling waves, and will never have another suitor.'

166

WAINAMOINEN'S EXPEDITION AND THE BIRTH OF THE KANTELE (HARP)

WAINAMOINEN reflected on what Ilmarinen had said of the prosperity of the Northland, and at length proposed that they should go and capture the Sampo and bring it back to Kalevala. But Ilmarinen said: 'It will be hard to carry off the Sampo, for Louhi has fastened it with nine great locks, and around it grow three roots, beneath the mountain and the waters and the sands.'

Still Wainamoinen persuaded him to go, and Ilmarinen went to his smithy and began to forge a sword for Wainamoinen. And when it was finished, it was so strong, by the power of the magic spells that had been used in making it, that it would cut through the hardest flint stones.

Then the two heroes put on their armour p. 174 and made their sledges ready, and drove off along the seashore northward. But they had not gone far before they heard a voice lamenting. They drove up to the spot whence the voice seemed to come, and there they found a ship lying deserted on the sands.

Wainamoinen asked the ship what it was lamenting over, and the ship replied: 'Alas, I weep because I am obliged to remain here idle; for I was built to be a warship, and I long to sail filled with warriors against the foe, but I am left here to lie alone and rot to pieces.' Then Wainamoinen said: 'Thou shalt lie here no longer, but we will sail in thee against the men of Pohjola. But tell me whether thou art a magic ship that can sail without wind, or oarsmen, or pilot.' 'Nay,' the ship replied, 'I cannot sail if the wind or oars do not help me on and some one guide me with the rudder. But give me these to help me, and I can sail faster than any other ship in the world.'

Then they left their sledges and launched the ship and stepped aboard. And Wainamoinen began to sing his wondrous spells, and in an instant one side of the vessel was filled with bearded warriors, and the other with lovely maids, and in the middle came powerful gray-bearded heroes. First he set the young men at the oars, but however hard they strove they could not budge the p. 175 ship. And next the maidens tried, but they too failed. Last of all the mighty gray-bearded heroes took the oars, but yet the vessel did not move. Then Ilmarinen himself grasped the oars, and in a moment the vessel was moving through the waters at full speed, with old Wainamoinen at the helm.

They had not gone far when they came to an island, and on the shore was a man working on a fishing-boat. As they drew nearer he looked up and hailed them, asking whither they were bound. Wainamoinen answered: 'O stupid Lemminkainen, dost thou not recognise us, and canst thou not guess whither we are bound?' Then Lemminkainen, for it was really he, said: 'I recognise you both now. It is Ilmarinen who is rowing, and thou art Wainamoinen. But tell me whither ye are sailing?'

Then Wainamoinen told him that they were bound for Pohjola to capture the magic Sampo, and, on hearing this, Lemminkainen begged to go with them, saying that he would fight valiantly with them. So they took him on board, and the three great heroes sailed on their way. But before they had gone much farther, they came to a place where there were lovely maidens singing sweetly on the shore, but all around were hidden rocks and whirlpools, and their vessel was near sinking. But Lemminkainen knew the spell that would compel the p. 176 maidens to calm the whirlpools, and to lead the ship in safety past all the hidden reefs out into open water again. And when Lemminkainen had sung this spell, old Wainamoinen was able to steer in safety through the foam-covered rocks and out into open water; but no sooner were they clear than the vessel stopped as suddenly as if she were anchored to the spot.

Ilmarinen and Lemminkainen then plunged a long pole to the bottom of the waters, and strove to push the ship ahead, but it was impossible. Then Wainamoinen bade Lemminkainen look beneath the vessel to see what it was that stopped them, and they found that it was no hidden reef or sand-bar, but a mighty pike on whose shoulders the vessel had stuck fast. At Wainamoinen's order, Lemminkainen drew his sword and aimed a mighty blow at the monster, but he missed it and fell overboard. He was drawn out all dripping, and the others consoled him for his failure. Next Ilmarinen drew his sword and struck at the monster, but at the first blow his sword broke in pieces. At last Wainamoinen, reproaching the others for their feebleness, drew his magic sword, and with one thrust he impaled the monster on it. Then lifting the monster out of the water he cut him into pieces and let them fall on the water, and float in towards land. p. 177

Thus the vessel was free at last. But the heroes were weary with their exertions, and so they rowed in to land, and there gathered up the fragments of the fish that had floated to the shore. Wainamoinen handed these pieces to the maidens who were with them in the vessel, and they prepared the most delicious feast from the pike, having enough and to spare for all on board. And they piled the bones in a heap on the rocks.

Then Wainamoinen looked at the pile of bones, and after pondering deeply he said: 'Wondrous things may be made from these bones, if only I can find a skilful workman to carry out my designs and make the *kantele*.' [5] But no workman could be found who was wise enough to understand Wainamoinen's directions, for no one had ever heard of a *kantele* before. At length old Wainamoinen saw that there was no one who could help him, and so he set to work himself. He made the arches of the harp from the pike's jawbones, and the pins that hold the strings he made from the teeth, and for the strings he took hairs from the tail of a magic steed.

[5] A sort of harp that is sometimes used even now in Finland. Pronounced *kan-tay-lay*. It usually has five strings.

And at last the *first kantele* was finished, and it was so beautiful that every one crowded round to look at it. When it was p. 178 all ready Wainamoinen handed it to those around to try their skill, but they could only make discords whenever they touched it. Then Lemminkainen bade the others leave it to him, for *he* would show them how to play upon it. But when he touched the strings it sounded worse than when any of the others had tried it. And after one and all had tried it, and found that it only gave forth discords, they proposed to throw it into the sea. But the harp said: 'I shall never perish in the sea, but will bring great joy to Kalevala. Put me in my maker's hands, and I will sing for him.' So they took it and laid it at the aged Wainamoinen's feet.

Then the great magician took the wondrous kantele and rested it upon his knee. First he tuned it, tightening all the strings until they sounded sweetly together, and then he swept his hands across them, and a flood of wonderful melody poured forth from the kantele. And as the wondrous notes resounded in the air, every living thing that heard them stopped and listened. From the forests came the bears and ermines, and the wolves and lynxes. Even Tapio the forest-god drew near, with all his attendant spirits, enchanted by the magic sounds. From the sea the fishes came to the edge of the waters, and the sea-god Ahto with his water-spirits. The daughters of the Sun and Moon stopped their spinning on the p. 179 clouds, and dropped their spindles, so that the threads were broken in two.

For three whole days the magic kantele poured forth its melody beneath Wainamoinen's skilful fingers, until every one that heard it wept, and even the master-player himself was at last moved to tears by the power of his own playing. The bright teardrops flowed down his long beard and over his garments, and on over the earth in sparkling streams, until they were lost in the waters of the deep sea. And then the music ceased, and Wainamoinen laid the kantele aside and said: 'Is there any one here who can gather up my teardrops from the sea?' But all were silent, for they could not do it.

But a raven came flying up and offered to attempt it, and Wainamoinen promised him the most beautiful plumage if he should succeed, but the raven tried and failed. Then came a duck, and Wainamoinen made it the same promise. And the duck swam off and dived down to the ocean's depths, and at length it had collected every teardrop and brought them to the great magician, but a wondrous change had taken place in them, for they were no longer tears, but the most beautiful pearls.

Thus were pearls first created, and for this the blue duck received its lovely plumage.

p. 180

'That is the loveliest story of all,' cried Mimi. 'How I wish I could have heard Wainamoinen's music! Was his kantele like the one pappa has up in the loft, Pappa Mikko? If it was, I wish pappa would play on ours.'

'I expect they are just alike,' replied Father Mikko; 'and when your pappa's pappa was alive, I remember that he used to play on the kantele very sweetly, but there are not many in our land that can play the kantele now.'

'Well,' said Mimi, with a sigh, 'I suppose there aren't, so you might as well tell us what Wainamoinen did next, Pappa Mikko, please.'

And Father Mikko began again.

A WATERFALL.

THE CAPTURE OF THE SAMPO

AFTER the magic kantele was finished, the three great heroes and magicians sailed away again towards the dismal Northland. Ilmarinen led the rowers on one side of the ship, and Lemminkainen on the other, and old Wainamoinen steered. They soon reached Pohjola and landed near Louhi's house.

When they had drawn their vessel up on land, they all went up to Louhi's house, and Wainamoinen told her that they were come for the Sampo; that if she would only give them the many-coloured lid they would go away content, but if not, they would take the whole Sampo by force. Then Louhi grew very angry and called together all the Northland warriors to slay them. But Wainamoinen began to play upon his kantele, and so wonderfully sweet were the p. 182 tunes that he played, that the warriors forgot all about fighting and began to weep, and all the maidens of Pohjola began to dance. Still Wainamoinen played on and on, until a deep slumber came upon all the Northland folk. Then he ceased playing, and cast a powerful spell over them, so that they should not awake.

When all the Pohjola folk were sound asleep the three great heroes went to the mountains to seek the magic Sampo. And as they went Wainamoinen played such wonderful music that the great cliffs opened before them, and left them an open road to where the Sampo lay hid. When they had come near the cavern in which the Sampo lay, they sent Lemminkainen to enter the cave and bring it out. He, boasting of his strength, went into the cavern, and seizing hold of the magic Sampo, he put forth all his strength to lift it up, but it remained immovable, for the roots had grown deep into the earth, and bound it down tightly.

Then Lemminkainen remembered a huge ox that he had seen out in the fields, with horns seven fathoms long, and he went after it and hitched it to the biggest plough he could find, and began to plough all around the roots which held the Sampo down. And in a very short while the roots became loosened, and they were able to pick up the p. 183 magic Sampo and carry it on board their vessel.

As soon as it was safely on board they sailed away, leaving all the Pohjola folk sleeping. On they flew towards their homes in Kalevala; but Lemminkainen grew weary of the silence, and asked Wainamoinen why he would not sing to cheer them. But Wainamoinen answered that song would only disturb the rowers, and that it was best never to rejoice until all danger was past. At length, when they had gone three days on their journey, Lemminkainen grew angry at Wainamoinen's silence, and began to sing himself. But his voice sounded harsh and unmelodious, and it made the very ship tremble.

Far off on the land a crane was standing amidst the rushes, amusing itself by counting its toes. But when it heard Lemminkainen's attempts at singing, it was so frightened that it flew off screaming over Pohjola, and by its screeching it awoke all the slumbering people. As soon as Louhi awoke she hurried off to her barns and cattle-pens to see if anything had been stolen, but she found everything all right. Next she hurried to the mountains, to the cavern where she had hidden the Sampo, but when she came there she found the cavern empty, and saw how her visitors had torn the Sampo loose from its fastenings. p. 184

Then Louhi returned to her house pale with anger and fear, for she knew that if the Sampo were lost that all the prosperity of the Northland would be lost with it. So she called up the goddess of the fogs, and sent her out to delay Wainamoinen's vessel. And then she called on Iko-Turso—a wicked monster living in the depths of the sea—to swim to the ship and sink it, and to eat the men in it, but to bring back the Sampo to Pohjola once more. And she prayed, moreover, to great Ukko that if the sea-monster should not succeed, that Ukko himself would send a fearful tempest to wreck the vessel.

First came the goddess of the fog, and wrapped them in such a thick mist that they could not move. Three days they lay so, and then Wainamoinen drew his sword, exclaiming: 'We shall all perish here in the fog if no attempt is made to drive it away,' and with these words he struck the waves with his sword. From the blade there flowed a stream of honey, and all at once the fog broke up, and left the way clear before them. But scarcely had the fog disappeared than they heard a mighty roaring sound, and the foam began to shoot up from the water alongside, and to cover the ship. Then Wainamoinen leaned over the vessel's side, and stretching out his arm he grasped something that he saw in the water, and pulled up the awful monster Iko-Turso. But p. 185 the monster was so affrighted by being lifted out of the water that he promised to leave them in peace, and never to appear above the waters again if Wainamoinen would only release him. So Wainamoinen let him go, and the second danger was past.

But now came the third and most terrible of all, for Ukko sent a mighty storm-wind, which lashed the waves into a fury, and stirred up the ocean to its very bottom. And at the very first pitch of the ship the magic kantele was swept overboard by the waves, and Ahto, the sea-god, caught it and carried it off to his home beneath the waves. Then Wainamoinen began to bewail the loss of his wonderful instrument; but as the storm grew worse, and tossed their ship about like a feather, all on board began to despair of ever reaching land alive. But Wainamoinen gave them comfort and courage, and he and Ilmarinen and Lemminkainen by their magic spells quietened the winds and the waves, and repaired the damage which the vessel had suffered from the storm. And then they went on their way in peace.

THE SAMPO IS LOST IN THE SEA

BUT when Louhi found that all her magic had failed, she assembled all her warriors, and embarked them in her largest ship, and herself sailed off to recapture the Sampo by force of arms. Before long they came in sight of Wainamoinen's vessel, and when he saw that Louhi was pursuing him with such a mighty host of warriors, he cried out to Ilmarinen and Lemminkainen to row with all their might, in order to escape from their pursuers. So all the rowers rowed until the vessel fairly trembled, and the foam was tossed up from the bow as high as the clouds, but still they could not gain on their pursuers.

Then Wainamoinen saw that he must use some other means, so he took out a piece of flint from his tinder-box and dropped it into the water, saying as he did so: 'Rise p. 187 up from the bottom of the sea into a mighty mountain, so that Louhi's ship may be dashed to pieces.' And suddenly a mountain of rock sprang up out of the water, and before Louhi could stop her ship it had hit upon the rocks and was wrecked.

But Louhi was not to be outdone in magic, so she took the timbers of the ship and made from them a magic eagle, using the rudder for its tail and five sharp iron scythes for its talons. And on his wings and back she posted all her warriors, and then the magic eagle rose up into the air. It made one circle round the heavens, and then lit upon the mast of Wainamoinen's vessel, almost overturning it by its weight. Wainamoinen first prayed to Ukko for aid, and then he asked Louhi if she would consent now to divide the Sampo between them. But she scorned his offer, and the eagle made a swoop downward to pick up the Sampo in its talons. But Lemminkainen raised his sword, and no sooner had the eagle grasped the Sampo than he brought down his sword with such force that every talon was cut off but one.

179

Then the eagle flew up on to the mast once more, and upbraided Lemminkainen because he had broken his promise to his mother that he would not go to war for sixty years. But Wainamoinen, believing that his last hour was come, took the rudder p. 188 in his hand and struck the eagle such a mighty blow that all the warriors fell from its wings and back into the water. Then the eagle made one more swoop down upon the vessel, and, with the one talon it had left, it dragged the Sampo over the side of the ship so that it fell to the bottom of the ocean and was broken to pieces. And it is this that has brought so much wealth to the sea, for where the Sampo is there will always be wealth also. But a few pieces of the lid floated ashore to Kalevala, and it is therefore that our country has now the harvests that before that grew in the dismal Northland.

But Louhi threatened Wainamoinen, saying: 'I will steal away thy silver moonlight and thy golden sunlight. I will send the frost and hail to kill thy crops, and will send the bear—Otso—from the forests to kill thy cattle and sheep. I will send upon thy people nine diseases, each one of them more fatal than the one before.' Then Wainamoinen replied: 'No one from dismal Northland can harm us of Kalevala, Only Ukko rules the fate of peoples, and he will guard my crops from frost and hail, and my cattle from the bear, Otso. Thou mayst hide evil people in thy Northland caverns, but thou canst never steal the Sun and Moon, and all thy frosts and plagues and bears may turn against thyself.' p. 189

And then Louhi departed to her home, weeping for the loss of the magic Sampo, and ever since that time there have been famines and poverty in gloomy Pohjola. But Wainamoinen and the other heroes returned home rejoicing, and on the shore they found fragments of the Sampo's lid. Then Wainamoinen prayed to Ukko to be merciful and kind to them, and to protect them from frost and hail and bears, and to let the golden light of the Moon and Sun shine for ever on the plains of Kalevala.

'Ah!' said Erik, half smiling, 'it's a great pity that the whole Sampo didn't float ashore to our country, for perhaps then there would never have been any famines in our land at all,' and he sighed as he thought of some of the hard winters in years past.

'All is in God's hands,' said Father Mikko reverently, 'and we must take both good and ill as they come to us—it is not for us to say what we would wish. Let us be thankful that even a part of the Sampo floated hither,' he added, smiling.

There was a few moments' silence, and then Mimi asked what Wainamoinen had done about his lost kantele, so Father Mikko went on.

THE BIRTH OF THE SECOND KANTELE

WHEN the heroes had returned home, and found the fragments of the Sampo on the shore, they wished to make merry over the good fortune which even these fragments were sure to bring, but Wainamoinen could not give them music, since the wondrous kantele had been lost in the sea. Then he bade Ilmarinen make a huge rake with copper teeth a hundred fathoms long and the handle a thousand fathoms, and when the rake was ready, Wainamoinen took it, and sailing out over the sea in a magic vessel that needed neither sails nor oars to move it, he raked over the whole bottom of the ocean. But he only raked up shells and seaweed, and found no trace of the kantele.

Then Wainamoinen returned sadly home, saying: 'Never again shall I pour forth p. 191 floods of music to the people of Kalevala from the magic strings of my kantele.' And driven on by his grief he left his house and went far off into the forest. As he wandered there he heard the birch-tree lamenting, and Wainamoinen asked the tree why it was unhappy when it had such lovely silver leaves and tassels. To this the birch-tree replied: 'Thou thinkest that I am always happy, and that my leaves and tassels must always be whispering joy. But, alas! I am so weak and feeble, and must always stand alone without a word of sympathy. Others rejoice at the coming of the spring, but I am robbed of bark and tassels and tender twigs, and am cut up for firewood, and then in the winter time the frost and the cold biting winds kill my young shoots and strip me of my silver leaves and leave me cold and naked.'

While the birch-tree was speaking, Wainamoinen's face began to brighten, and he finally exclaimed: 'Weep no more, good birch-tree, for I will turn thy grief into joy and make thee sing the most marvellous songs.' Having said this he set to work to make a new kantele, taking birch-wood for the framework. At length the frame was all ready, but he did not know of what to make the pegs. Suddenly he came upon a great oak-tree on which grew golden-coloured acorns, and on each acorn sat a p. 192 sacred cuckoo singing its melody. So Wainamoinen took a piece of the oak and made the pegs from it.

But the harp was not yet finished, for the five strings were still lacking. Then Wainamoinen journeyed on through the forest, until at length he came to where a forest-maiden was sitting on a mound and singing, and her long golden hair was falling loose over her shoulders. So Wainamoinen went up to her and begged her to give him some of her golden tresses, from which to weave the five strings for the kantele. And the maiden willingly gave up a portion of her golden hair, and from it Wainamoinen wove five strings, and at last the second kantele was complete. Then Wainamoinen sat down upon a rock and placed the kantele upon his knees, and after putting all the strings in tune he began to play. The fairy music resounded over hill and dale, until at length the very mountains began to dance with delight, and the rocks were rent in sunder and floated on the surface of the ocean. The trees of the forest, too, laughed with joy and began to dance about like children. The young men and maidens rejoiced as they listened to the music, and the gray-haired men and women were amazed, while the babies tried to crawl to where the sweet sounds came from.

The magic music resounded far and wide p. 193 over Kalevala, and all the wild beasts of the forest fell upon their knees in wonder, while the birds perched upon the trees about him and accompanied the music with their singing. The fish left their homes beneath the waters and crowded to the shore to listen. And everything in nature, from earth and air and water, came to listen to the magic sweetness of Wainamoinen's playing.

Three days and more he played unceasing; playing in the houses of his people until their very beams rejoiced, and wandering through the forest, where the trees all bent in homage to him and waved their branches to his music. Then over the meadows, still playing, until the very ferns and flowers laughed with delight and the bushes chimed in in unison with the magic music of the kantele.

'Oh! I'm so glad that he got another kantele,' cried little Mimi, delighted. 'And now what is coming next, Pappa Mikko?'

'I shall tell you all of Louhi's attempt at revenge on the heroes who captured the Sampo,' he replied; 'and how they all failed, and then I shall wind up with the last story of all!'

After having rested a while, the old man continued.

LOUHI ATTEMPTS REVENGE

LOUHI grew more and more angry and envious when she heard how prosperous and happy all the folk of Kalevala were, since the fragments of the Sampo had floated to their shore. So she pondered long in her evil heart, how she might send them sorrow and misfortune. Now just at that time the old witch Lowjatar, Tuoni's daughter, came to Louhi and asked for shelter from the storms and cold, and Louhi took her in and treated her like an honoured guest. And while Lowjatar was there, nine children were born to her, all horrible diseases, and she named them Colic, Fever, Plague, Pleurisy, Ulcer, Consumption, Gout, Sterility, and Cancer. And then Louhi's evil heart rejoiced, and she took the nine diseases and sent them into Kalevala, there to harass and kill Wainamoinen's people.

p. 195

And when the diseases came, every one in Kalevala, both young and old, fell ill of all sorts of illnesses, and Wainamoinen at first did not know whence all this evil had come. But soon by his magic power he learned that it came from the children of Tuoni's daughter, Lowjatar, and then he set to work to drive them away. First he took all those that were ill to the bath-houses, and then he brought buckets of water and heated blocks of stone until he had filled the whole room with warm steam. Then he prayed to Ukko to drive away all these diseases from them, and to send these evil spirits to Tuoni's kingdom, where they belonged.

After Wainamoinen had prayed thus to Ukko, he took a magic balsam and rubbed it over all those that were ill, and sang magic spells over them, and then prayed once more to Ukko for success, and at length he drove out the nine diseases and saved his people from dying.

When the nine diseases had been driven out of Kalevala, the news of Wainamoinen's victory over them came at length to the old witch Louhi, and she grew angrier than ever that her revenge had failed. But she pondered over what means of revenge she should try next, and at length she hit upon another plan. She went out into the forest and cast a magic spell upon the hugest bear p. 196 in all the North-land—the great Otso [6]—and he hastened from his Pohjola home and began to kill the flocks and herds in Kalevala.

[6] *Otso* = bear.

Then Wainamoinen hastened to Ilmarinen, and bade him make a triple-pointed spear with which to kill Otso. And when the spear was ready, Wainamoinen hastened off to the forest to find the bear, singing as he went, and calling upon the forest-god Tapio and his wife to grant him success in his hunt. He had not gone far before he heard his dog bark, and hurrying up to the spot he found Otso standing facing the dog and trying to snap him up, and before the bear perceived him, Wainamoinen was able to end Otso's life with a single thrust of his magic spear.

When Otso was dead, Wainamoinen threw the body across his shoulder and hastened off home, singing songs of rejoicing as he went. And when he reached his house there was great rejoicing, and every one came out to welcome the dead bear, addressing it as if Otso were some honoured guest come to see them. First Wainamoinen sang a song of praise to the dead Otso, and bade his people welcome him with all due honour. And then the people answered with the most extravagant expressions of pleasure and welcome and p. 197 admiration for Otso, and offered him all the best things in the house, and when all this ceremony was over they took off the fur and cut the body up ready for cooking, and pre-pared the steaks and joints to make a grand feast.

At length the whole of the bear was cooked, and a great feast was spread in Wainamoinen's house on golden dishes, and with spar-kling beer in copper beakers. And when all were seated at the table, Wainamoinen rose and sang the story of Otso's birth and life. And this is the story which he sang: 'Long ago a maiden walked in the ether on the edges of the clouds, and as she walked she threw down wool and hair upon the waters from two boxes that she carried. The wool and hair were floated in to the shore, and there Mielikki, wife of the forest-god, found them and joined the wool and hair together by magic spells. Then she laid the bundle in a birch-bark basket and bound it in the top of the lofty pine, and there the young bear was rocked into life.

'Otso grew quickly and became graceful in his movements, although his feet were clumsy and his ankles crooked, his mouth large and forehead broad; but he still had no teeth or claws. Then Mielikki said: "I would give thee claws and teeth, Otso, but I fear that thou wilt use them to harm p. 198 people with." But Otso fell on his knees and swore that he would never harm the good. So Mielikki took the hardest knots from all the trees to make him teeth and claws, but all of them were too weak. Then she went to a magic fir that grew in Tapio's kingdom, and which had silver branches and golden cones, and from these she made Otso's claws and teeth. Thus was Otso born and reared.'

So they feasted and made merry, and when the feast was over they all tried to see which could pull out Otso's teeth and claws, in order to preserve them for their magic power. And of all the men there only the aged Wainamoinen could draw them out. When this was done, Wainamoinen called for his kantele and bade them light torches, as it was already dark. Then he sang sweet songs and played lovely music, so that the long evening passed away like magic, and he sang of the hunter's victory and prayed to Ukko always to give good fortune to the hunters of Kalevala.

Thus were Louhi's two first attempts at revenge unsuccessful.

LOUHI STEALS THE SUN, THE MOON, AND FIRE

WHEN these two dangers were overcome, Wainamoinen played upon his kantele so sweetly that the Sun and Moon came down from their stations in the sky to listen to his music. But evil Louhi crept upon them unawares and made both Sun and Moon her captives, and carried them off to the dismal Northland, and there she hid them both in caverns in the mountains, that they might never again shine upon Kalevala. Next Louhi crept back to Kalevala and stole all the fire from the hearths, and left all their homes cold and cheerless. Then there was nothing but black night in the world, and great Ukko himself did not know what to do without the light of the Sun and Moon.

Ukko wandered all over the clouds to find p. 200 out what had become of the Sun and Moon, and at last he whirled his fire-sword round his head so that the lightning flashed over the whole sky. From this lightning he kindled a little fire, and putting it in a gold and silver cradle, he gave it to the Ether-maidens to rock and care for, until it grew into a second Sun. So the Fire-child was cared for tenderly, and he grew fast; but one day the maidens were not watching him closely, and he escaped from them, and bursting through the clouds with a noise like a thunder-clap, he shot across the heavens like a red fire-ball.

Then Wainamoinen said to Ilmarinen: 'Come, let us see what this fire is that is fallen from the heavens.' And so they set out towards the spot where the ball of fire had seemed to fall. Soon they came to a wide river and set to work to make a magic boat to cross it, and in a very short time the boat was made, and they rowed over. On the other bank they were met by the oldest of the Ether-maidens, who asked them whither they were going.

So they told her who they were, and that they had lost all fire and light in Kalevala, so that they were come to seek the fire that they had seen fall from the heavens. Then the Ether-maiden told them what had happened, saying: 'After the Fire-child had begun to grow, he escaped from us one day p. 201 and bursting through the clouds he came down to Pohjola. There he killed youths and babes and old people, until he was driven away by a magic spell. He fled thence, burning fields and forests on his way, until at length he plunged into a great lake, and made the waters boil and rage. Then the fish held a council how to get rid of him, and it was decided that one of them must swallow him. First the salmon tried, but failed, and then the bold whiting made a dash and succeeded in swallowing the evil Fire-child. After this the waters of the lake grew quiet, and all went on as before.

'But soon the whiting was seized with terrible pains and began to swim round in agony, begging for some one to kill him and put him out of his sufferings. For a long time he swam about unheeded, but at last a trout seized the whiting and swallowed him. For a while all was quiet again, but then the trout began to suffer in his turn. Still every fish was afraid to swallow him, until a pike darted up and ate up the trout. But then the pike was seized with the same pains, and he is now swimming about in great agony, but none will help him.'

When the Ether-maiden had finished her account of what had happened, Wainamoinen and Ilmarinen wove a great net from sea-weed, and hurrying to the lake they p. 202 began to draw the net all through it in order to catch the Fire-fish. But the net was a poor one, and they failed to catch the pike that had swallowed the other fish and the Fire-child.

Then the two magicians gave up their useless net, and, choosing an island near by, they resolved to plant flax that they might make a stronger and better net. They went to Tuoni's kingdom before they could find the proper seed, and found it there under the care of a tiny insect. When they had brought the seed from the Deathland, they planted it on the shore, in the ashes of a ship that had been burnt there, and in a single night the flax had grown up and ripened. Then they pulled it, and washed and dried and combed it, and took it to the Kalevala maidens to spin. Soon the spinning was done and the net was woven.

So the two great heroes took the flaxen net and hastened back to the lake and began to drag for the Fire-fish. But they only caught common fish, and the pike remained hidden in the deep caverns. Then Wainamoinen made the net longer and wider and they tried again, but though they caught fish of every species, the Fire-fish was not amongst them. Wainamoinen then prayed to Ahto, god of the ocean, and his wife, Wellamo, that they would drive the p. 203 Fire-fish into his nets. Scarcely had Wainamoinen finished speaking, when a little dwarf rose from the waters and offered to help them. They accepted the tiny man's aid, and while they drew their nets, the dwarf beat the waters with a magic pole and scared all the fish toward them. And as they drew, Wainamoinen sang a magic charm to bring the fish in still greater numbers.

This time the net was full of pike, and they dragged it to the shore rejoicing, and among them they found the Fire-fish. So they threw the other fish back into the water, and Wainamoinen drew his knife and began to cut up the Fire-fish. Inside of the pike he found the trout, and inside of the trout the whiting, and on opening the whiting he came upon a ball of blue yarn. Wainamoinen quickly unwound the blue ball, and within that found a red ball, and when he had opened the red ball he came to the ball of fire in the middle.

They pondered how they should get the fire to Kalevala, and at last Ilmarinen seized it in his hands to carry it off. But it singed Wainamoinen's beard and burned Ilmarinen's hands dreadfully, and then it jumped out of their reach and rolled off over field and forest, burning everything in its course. Wainamoinen hastened after it, and at length caught it hidden in a mass of punk-wood. p. 204 Then he took it and put it, wood and all, in a copper box and hastened off home. Thus the fire returned to Kalevala.

But Ilmarinen, suffering great agony from his burnt hands, hastened to the sea to lave them in the cool water. And he called up the ice and frost and snow to come and cool his parched hands, and, when all these proved insufficient, he called on great Ukko to send him some healing balm to take away the cruel torture. And Ukko granted his prayer and his hands were healed. Then Ilmarinen re-

193

turned home and rejoiced to find that Wainamoinen had already brought the fire thither.

THE RESTORATION OF THE SUN AND MOON

 THOUGH the Fire had been restored to Kalevala, still the golden Moon and the silver Sun were lost, and the frost came and killed the crops, and the cattle began to die of hunger. Every living thing felt sick and faint in the dark, dreary world. Then one of the maidens of Kalevala suggested to Ilmarinen to make a moon of gold and a sun of silver, and to hang them up in the heavens; so Ilmarinen set to work. While he was forging them, Wainamoinen came and asked what he was working at, and so Ilmarinen told him that he was going to make a new sun and moon. But Wainamoinen said: 'This is mere folly, for silver and gold will not shine like the sun and moon.' Still Ilmarinen worked on, and at length he had forged a moon of gold p. 206 and a sun of silver, and hung them in their places in the sky. But they gave no light, as Wainamoinen had said.

Then Wainamoinen determined to find out where the sun and moon had gone. So he cut three chips from an alder-tree, and laying them on the ground before him, he cast many magic spells over them. Then when all was ready, he asked the alder-chips to tell him truly where the sun and moon were hid. The alder-chips then answered, that they were hidden in the caverns of the mountains of Pohjola.

No sooner had Wainamoinen heard this, than he made ready for a journey and started off for the dismal Northland. When he had travelled three days and was come to the borders of Pohjola, he found a wide river in the road and no boat to cross over in. So he built a huge fire on the shore, and soon such a dense column of smoke arose that Louhi sent some one to see what was the matter. But when Wainamoinen called to the messenger to bring him a boat, the man made no reply, but hurried back to Louhi and told her that it was Wainamoinen, who was coming to her house.

Then Wainamoinen saw that he could never get across in that way, so he changed himself into a pike and swam over very easily, and then changed back to his own p. 207 shape when he had reached the opposite shore. He hastened on with mighty strides, and soon reached Louhi's dwelling. There he was met as if he were a most honoured guest, and they invited him into the hall. Wainamoinen went in unsuspectingly, but no sooner was he inside than he found himself surrounded by crowds of armed warriors.

The warriors asked him in a threatening tone why he had come thither. But Wainamoinen was not frightened, but answered boldly that he had come to seek the Sun and the Moon. Then the chief of the warriors replied: 'We have the Sun and Moon safe in a mountain cavern, and thou shalt never get them back, nor shalt thou leave this hall alive.' No sooner had he finished speaking than Wainamoinen drew his magic sword, and fell upon those that stood between him and the door. They gave way before him, and in a moment he was out in the courtyard, where he could have room to fight fairly. All the warriors rushed at him with drawn swords and lifted spears, and the fire flashed from their weapons. But Wainamoinen was more than a match for all of them, and in a very short time he had stretched them all lifeless on the ground.

Then he left the court and hastened on to find the Sun and Moon. Soon he came p. 208 to a solitary birch-tree, and beside the tree stood a carved pillar of stone, which concealed an opening in the rocks. Wainamoinen gave three blows with his magic sword, and the pillar broke in pieces, showing behind it an entrance into the rock; but the entrance was shut by a massive door, and there was only a little crack through which he could peep. Inside he saw the Sun and Moon prisoners, but though he tried with all his strength and all his magic spells to open the door, it still remained tightly shut, and he could not budge it so much as an inch.

Wainamoinen began to despair of ever succeeding in liberating the Sun and Moon, and he hastened off home to ask for Ilmarinen's help. He directed him to forge a whole set of skeleton-keys, so that some one of them would fit the lock of the door to the Sun's prison. Ilmarinen went to work and soon his anvil was ringing merrily to the blows of his hammer.

Now Louhi had grown very much alarmed after Wainamoinen had slain all her warriors, and so she assumed the shape of an eagle and flew away to Kalevala to see what was going on there. She heard the merry ring of Ilmarinen's work and flew down and lit in the window of the smithy. There she asked what he was doing, and the cunning Ilmarinen replied: 'I am forging a collar p. 209 of steel for the neck of evil Louhi, and with it I shall bind her fast to the rocks.'

Louhi was terribly alarmed at this, so she flew off to Pohjola and released the Sun and Moon from prison immediately, and sent them up to their places in the heavens. Then the silver sunlight and the golden moonlight returned once more to Kalevala, and Ilmarinen, and Wainamoinen, and all the people offered up a prayer that they might never again be deprived of the blessed Sun and Moon.

'It would have served old Louhi right if Ilmarinen *had* made a steel collar and put it round her neck,' said Mimi. 'But I'm so glad that Wainamoinen always got the best of it,' she added.

'There was one time when he was defeated, however,' said Father Mikko, 'and now I shall tell it you. It is the last story, and is about Wainamoinen's departure from Kalevala.' So he began.

MARIATTA AND WAINAMOINEN'S DEPARTURE

THERE lived a fair and lovely maiden in Kalevala, called Mariatta. She was the loveliest and purest of virgins, and tended her parents' flocks upon the mountain sides. Here one day, as she was watching the sheep, she heard a voice calling to her, and on looking round she found that it was a bright red berry calling to her, and asking her to pluck it. Mariatta did not know that this was a magic berry, so she picked it and put it to her lips to eat it. But the berry rolled from her lips down into her bosom, and said to her: 'Thou shalt have a son, and he shall become a mighty man and drive forth the old magician Wainamoinen.'

Then Mariatta took the flocks home and was so silent and still that her parents p. 211 noticed it and asked her what was the matter. So she told them what had happened, but they grew angry and would not keep her in their house, for they did not believe the story about the berry.

Poor Mariatta was now obliged to wander about without a shelter from the cold winds. At length she sent a servant, who had remained faithful to her and had accompanied her, to a village of Pohjola to ask for shelter from an old man named Ruotus. The maid, Piltti, went to Ruotus and told him of Mariatta's hard lot, but Ruotus and his wife would not have her in their house, but only grudgingly consented to let her go to a stable in the forest, where the Fire-horse of Hisi was kept.

So Mariatta was obliged to go to the stable in the dense forest far off from every human being, and there she begged the Hisi-horse to keep her warm by his fiery breath. The Hisi-horse was kinder to her than men had been, for he let her lie down comfortably in his manger, and kept her warm with his fiery breath. There the babe was born, and his mother grew happy once more, in spite of her sorrowful circumstances. But one night, while she slept, the babe disappeared, and the poor mother was overwhelmed with grief.

Then she wandered forth and looked everywhere for him, but in vain. So she p. 212 asked the North-star if he had seen her son. But the North-star answered: 'I would not tell thee even if I knew. For it is thy son who hath made me and set me here in the bitter cold.' And next Mariatta asked the Moon, and received the same answer as the North-star had given. Then she went to the Sun and asked him. And the Sun said: 'I know very well where thy son is hidden, for he made me and put me here to shine with my silver light. He lies sleeping yonder in the Swampland.' So Mariatta hastened to the spot that the Sun had pointed out and there found her babe sleeping peacefully in the water among the rushes.

Then she returned with the babe to her father's house, and this time he received her and allowed her to live there in peace. And the child grew in beauty and wisdom, and his mother called him Flower, but others called him Son-of-Sorrow. Then his mother called in an old man, Wirokannas, to baptize the child, but Wirokannas said: 'First must some one see if the child shall become an honest man, or a wicked wizard, for if he be not honest I will not baptize him.'

So Wainamoinen was called to examine the child—it was only two weeks old then—and see if it would grow up a noble man or not. Wainamoinen came and saw the p. 213 child, and then said: 'Since this child is only a poor outcast, born in a manger, and having no father save a berry, let him be cast out on to the hillsides or into the marshes to perish.'

But all at once the babe himself began to speak, saying: 'O aged Wainamoinen, foolish hero, thou hast given a false decision. Thou thyself hast done great wrongs, yet hast not been punished. Thou gavest thine own brother Ilmarinen to ransom thy poor life. Thou persecuted the lovely Aino so that she perished in the deep sea, yet thou wert not killed for all this.'

Then Wirokannas saw that this was truly a magic babe, and he baptized him to become a mighty hero, and a ruler and king over Kalevala.

Years passed by after this, and Wainamoinen felt his power gradually leaving him and going over to Mariatta's child. So the ancient hero, with a sad heart, sang his last magic spell in Kalevala, and made a magic boat of copper to sail away in. Then he cast loose from the shore and sailed off towards the west, singing as he went: 'Fare ye well, my people. Many suns shall rise and set on Kalevala until the people shall at length regret my absence and shall call upon me to come back with my magic songs and wisdom. Fare ye well.'

Thus Wainamoinen, in his magic boat p. 214 of copper, left Kalevala. On he sailed to the land of the setting sun, and at length he reached the haven and anchored his boat, never again to return to Kalevala. But the wondrous kantele and all his songs and wisdom remain among us to this day.

'And now,' said Father Mikko, 'I have told you my last story—old Wainamoinen has left Kalevala and the rule of the Christ-child has begun. Under it our land has advanced and grown comfortable and happy—let us only pray that we may never be less so.'

They were all silent for some time, and then all of them thanked Father Mikko heartily for the pleasure that he had given them. Soon after this they had supper and went to bed, and the next morning Father Mikko drove off in his sledge, the moonlight covering all the country with a flood of silver, and soon he had disappeared into the dark and silent fir-forest; but not before he had promised them all that he would stop there again next year if possible.

THE END